NEW YORK REVIEW BOOKS
CLASSICS

FREE DAY

INÈS CAGNATI (1937–2007) was born in Monclar, France, in the Aquitaine region of Lot-et-Garonne, and died in Orsay. The child of Italian immigrants, she became a French citizen but never considered herself French. With a bachelor's degree in modern literature and a certificate for secondary-school instruction, she worked as a professor of literature at the Lycée Carnot in Paris. Cagnati was the author of four prize-winning books: *Le Jour de congé* (*Free Day*, 1973); *Génie la folle* (1976); *Mosé, ou Le Lézard qui pleurait* (1979); and *Les Pipistrelles* (1989).

LIESL SCHILLINGER is a literary critic, writer, and translator, and teaches journalism and criticism at the Eugene Lang College of Liberal Arts of the New School for Social Research in New York City. Her articles, reviews, and essays have appeared in *The New York Times, Foreign Policy, The New York Review of Books, The New Yorker, The Atlantic, The Washington Post*, and other publications. She has translated works by Alexandre Dumas *fils*, Nataša Dragnić, Jean Echenoz, and others, and is the author of *Wordbirds: An Irreverent Lexicon for the 21st Century*. In 2017 she was named a Chevalier of the Order of Arts and Letters of France.

D0972457

FREE DAY

INÈS CAGNATI

Translated from the French and with an introduction by
LIESL SCHILLINGER

NEW YORK REVIEW BOOKS

New York

THIS IS A NEW YORK REVIEW BOOK
PUBLISHED BY THE NEW YORK REVIEW OF BOOKS
435 Hudson Street, New York, NY 10014
www.nyrb.com

Originally published in the French language as *Le Jour de congé*.

Library of Congress Cataloging-in-Publication Data
Names: Cagnati, Inès, 1937–2007, author. | Schillinger, Liesl, translator, writer
   of introduction.
Title: Free day / Ines Cagnati ; translated and with an introduction by Liesl
   Schillinger.
Other titles: Jour de conge. English
Description: New York : New York Review Books, [2019] | Series: New York
   Review Books Classics
Identifiers: LCCN 2019017595 (print) | LCCN 2019018898 (ebook) | ISBN
   9781681373591 (epub) | ISBN 9781681373584 (paperback)
Subjects: | BISAC: FICTION / Contemporary Women. | FICTION / Coming
   of Age. | FICTION / Family Life.
Classification: LCC PQ2663.A334 (ebook) | LCC PQ2663.A334 J613 2019
   (print) | DDC 843/.914—dc23
LC record available at https://lccn.loc.gov/2019017595

ISBN 978-1-68137-358-4
Available as an electronic book; ISBN 978-1-68137-359-1

Printed in the United States of America on acid-free paper.
10 9 8 7 6 5 4 3 2 1

CONTENTS

INTRODUCTION

Free French

HOW DO you learn the stories of people who are too impoverished, powerless, or uneducated to write their stories themselves? Often it is outsiders who relay them, through leaps of empathetic imagination—as Harriet Beecher Stowe did with *Uncle Tom's Cabin*, awakening the conscience of the nation by exposing the cruelties of American slavery, or as Jane Wagner did with her 1969 children's book, *J. T.*, calling attention to the plight of the urban poor in a novella about a boy who rescues a stray cat whose miseries resemble his own. But sometimes, authors who have overcome daunting circumstances emerge from profoundly adverse environments to give voice to personal travails in their own words. The experiences they describe land in us with disturbing power and commanding authenticity. Consider Jeannette Walls's *The Glass Castle*, or Tara Westover's *Educated*. Inès Cagnati is such an author. Her novels and short stories about the Italian immigrant community in France in the middle of the twentieth century resurrect a transitional era that might otherwise have passed without leaving a trace. Her quietly devastating debut novel, *Free Day*, which won France's Prix Roger Nimier in 1973, offers an insider's view of what it feels like to be an outsider, not only in the land in which you live but in the family to which you were born.

In the last century, between the wars, an unprecedented

"massive" and "sudden" wave of immigration flooded the southern French region of Aquitaine. Eighty thousand Italians, mostly agricultural workers, moved to the severely underpopulated departments of Lot-et-Garonne and Midi-Pyrénées, lured by reports of plentiful jobs, gigantic tomatoes, and "dreams of El Dorado."* Illiterate for the most part and unable to speak French, many of these economic refugees found work on marshy, rocky farmland that had been abandoned by Frenchmen who had fallen in the Great War or who had moved to the city. The arrival of the Italians revived a failing region, but it also prompted French anxieties about alien invasion and cries for quotas. How did the French farmers in the region treat the economic refugees? How did the Italian newcomers treat one another? And what were the actual conditions of daily life in the tightly knit rural communities where the newcomers settled?

In 1997, a symposium in Bordeaux addressed these questions. The historians and sociologists in attendance concurred that Cagnati's "lucid and unsparing" fiction was an "indispensable" resource, and built upon it by soliciting oral histories of other first- and second-generation Italo-French southerners. They had plenty of statistics, of course (population figures and percentages), but to understand the *vécu*, the lived reality behind the numbers, the scholars needed to speak with individual men and women who remembered what it had been like to be a child in that time of privation, prejudice, and migration, because, as Cagnati writes, "A child is life's memory of itself." And for those stories to gain a

*From a study of the twentieth-century Italian immigration wave in southwestern France, "L'arrivée et l'implantation des Italiens dans le sud-ouest (1920–1939)" by Monique Rouch, in *Les Italiens en France de 1914 à 1940* (Rome: École Française de Rome, 1986).

human complexion, they needed names attached to them. "It's important for every thing to have its own name," Cagnati emphasized. When you name things, she explained, they become "less neglected, because once you give them a name, people can know them and talk about them." In *Free Day*, she gives names to the unnamed and voices to the voiceless. As in most of her later fictions, she tells her story from the point of view of a little girl—as helpless as the child narrator of François Truffaut's *The 400 Blows*—who relates her daily life without judgment and with brutal, unrestrained truthfulness that kindles pathos in the reader.

The story begins on a gelid, white-skied winter weekend in southern France in the 1950s. Fourteen-year-old Galla is cycling the twenty miles between the Catholic girls' school she attends, where she is scorned as an uncouth scholarship student and mocked for her ugly homemade clothing, and the remote hardscrabble farm where her family lives. Her parents had not wanted her to go to school at all; they needed her at home to do the work that her addled, worn-out, perpetually pregnant mother was no longer capable of doing. Galla has always been the family's workhorse, dressing, feeding, and looking after her four little sisters (especially the youngest, the angelic, blind, four-year-old Antonnella), minding the cattle, assisting at the birthing of calves, working in the fields, and deflecting the fury of her brutal father. But Galla, in an act of rebellion and self-preservation, stubbornly insists on pursuing her education.

She rides across the frigid, marshy, rocky landscape on a rusty, squealing bicycle that is her only reliable companion and support. The bike's wheels are caked with icy mud from the riverine path that laces through the fields, woods, and bogs that lie between the farm and the road to town. In summertime, Galla loves the untamed countryside, rejoicing at "the marshes . . . rustling with wild tulips, the fields and the ditches gone wild with flowers and all their mingled scents." But it is winter now, and the going is treacherous. The mud slows her down but she perseveres. Whenever the bike hits a patch of black ice and shoots off the asphalt, skidding down sleet-encrusted slopes towards the riverbank, Galla fears for the bike's safety, not her own. But she keeps going, "sometimes pedaling, sometimes getting off to gently guide my bicycle." She sees the bicycle as her friend. "I thought, I'm holding its hand. I would have liked to be able to sing to cheer us up, but I couldn't. I was too tired." This is a journey Galla usually makes every two weeks, from school to home and back, to comfort her mother, who weeps every time she leaves. But this particular journey cannot be repeated. The reasons why emerge through recollections and reveries that race through Galla's mind as she rides, some of them harsh and matter-of-fact, some of them fanciful dreams of lands "where the days are gilded with sunshine, where you sleep at night cradled in the blue of the waves of the sea." Like another unhappy literary child, Charlotte Brontë's Jane Eyre, Galla is in the position of all children, who can "feel, but they cannot analyze their feelings," and "know not how to express the result of the process in words."

Free Day reflects a good deal of the author's own history. Cagnati, who died in 2007, was born in the French town of Monclar-d'Agénais, in Lot-et-Garonne, in 1937. Her parents were both Italian—her father from Treviso, her mother from Vicenza—and she would never consider herself French. In one of her extremely rare television appearances, in 1989, upon the release of her final book, *Les Pipistrelles* (named for a species of bat common in southern France), speaking fluent French that retained an Italianate stamp, she told the moderator that, in her childhood, she and her family and their immigrant neighbors "had the misfortune of being foreigners, and always being regarded as strangers." "But... you're French," he said. "No," she said. She was naturalized, but not a citizen. "When my parents had me naturalized, that was a tragedy," she said, chain-smoking all the while, "because I was not French. I wasn't Italian anymore either. So I was nothing." "Was childhood a happy time for you?" asked the benighted moderator. "Completely unhappy," she said. She had grown up speaking Italian, and only learned French upon arriving at school. Like most of her protagonists, she had felt separate. "To be a child, it seems to me, is to be born apart," she said, because adults objectify children as something "little," something other. Children and the elderly (the subject of her 1979 novel, *Mosé, ou Le Lézard qui pleurait*—"Moses, or The Lizard That Cried") or "crazy people" (the subject of her 1977 novel *Génie la folle*) are "not like other people, they don't react like other people, they're not perceived to be like other people," she explained. Flailing for a scrap of comfort, the moderator protested, "But your anchor point, the value you hold to most firmly, seems to be the family unit." "Yes," she agreed, "because it's the only foothold you have in the world, the familial unit, with the father and the mother, even if they did not do for you what they could have done..."

Did she really feel like a foreigner, he asked, given her success on the French literary scene, her career as a professor of French, and her prizes? "Yes, always," she said. "Even now."

In her works, Cagnati often addresses the specific hardships faced by immigrant girls and women of her era, both in the wider society and in their own households. Barred from full inclusion in their new country, they also suffered in their villages and homes from a sexism that limited their freedoms, condoned violence against them, and blamed them if they were sexually attacked. In *Free Day*, Galla fears a sexual predator who lurks in the marshes near her home; she knows that if he attacks her or her sisters, it is they alone who will suffer, he will not be brought to justice. In an introduction to her novel *Génie la Folle*, about an outcast mother and daughter, Cagnati deplored the double standard. She wrote: "A girl who is raped, who didn't know how to protect her virtue outside of marriage, is seen as guiltier than the man who raped her; who, it is said, was only fulfilling his role as a male." She asks: "Where is common sense to be found?" Galla, for her part, does not ask that question; she simply accepts that this is how things are.

The scholars in Bordeaux buttressed their research and the oral histories they had collected with an interview Cagnati gave to a regional newspaper in 1984. In it, she spoke at length about the difficulties that she, like Galla, had encountered as an immigrant high-school student. "At school, my world turned upside down," Cagnati told the reporter. "I understood nothing that anyone told me, I couldn't even obey, I didn't know what they wanted." The French schoolchildren made fun of her. "Their world was hostile, aggressive, they didn't want us there. I didn't understand their language or their rules, or what I was supposed to do in order to be tolerated, or at least to be pardoned for being myself, different," she said. "I think it was the same for the others." She added, "I think we were rejected more because we were poor than because we were Italian." Cagnati's impressions were confirmed by the accounts of several of her immigrant contemporaries. "Nobody is meaner than kids, you know," said one. "You can't say they were mean," countered another, "but they considered us a little inferior. And because of our large families, they took us for, I'm not saying Gypsies, but close." Still, according to a third Italian transplant, on the whole, "we were appreciated for our goodwill, our hard work, and our honesty."

At a contemporary geopolitical moment when populist leaders across the globe are demonizing immigrants and outsiders, and when the xenophobic rhetoric and punitive, inhuman policies of President Donald Trump target the foreign-born, Cagnati's searing evocation of the immigrant experience in *Free Day* moves the heart and stirs the conscience. Where, indeed, is common sense to be found?

Cagnati was luckier than today's immigrants. In spite of the rough transition period that shaped her and some of her peers, the integration of the interwar Italian boom generations into the French community proceeded with remarkable smoothness. No anti-immigrant protests broke out in Lot-et-Garonne or Midi-Pyrénées; the Italians were needed, and over time, they were accepted, such that today young generations of Italian-descended French in the southwest don't question their nationality, their right to be French. Reading *Free Day*, they, like us, can understand the distance that their predecessors—like Galla, like Cagnati—traveled to earn their sense of belonging, their right to be themselves, their right to be free.

—LIESL SCHILLINGER

FREE DAY

TO MY SISTERS

ELSA

GILDA

ANNIE

ANABEL

Childhood, my love, was it only that?....
Childhood, my love! nothing to do but to yield...
—Saint-John Perse

I

I LEANED my bicycle against the wall of the barn and left it there. I could have kept on dragging it until it was in front of the house, as usual. It's not more than fifty yards. But I'd had enough of my bicycle. Of pedaling. Of pushing it. Of pedaling. Of pushing it. And, in the end, carrying it. Completely enough. I'd had it. Because all of that had been going on for three or four hours, maybe more, even, and there comes a point when things have gone on long enough, and you say: No.

On top of that, and as if by accident, a rain to end the world had been falling all those hours I was struggling with my bike. When I got home, it wasn't raining anymore. Things like that happen, I've often noticed, always bad timing. As for the rain, so much water had fallen on the earth in those few hours that the clouds must have completely dried up. No surprise, then, that the filthy rain had stopped.

Anyway, none of that mattered to me. When I'm at home, I like to listen to the rain coming down hard. Ever since I've been going to the high school, I like being at home, whether it's raining or nice out.

Of course, if I had my way, I would only like sunshine. The brightest sun. The most merciless. The kind whose weakest ray, touching the ground, opens broad cracks that cut deep into the heart of the earth. Under a sun like that, entire rivers dry up and disappear forever, drunk up by the sun. People, plants, animals, everything dies of thirst and of joy in the sun. Everything shines, rejoices, and dies. I'd like to live in a sunlit land like that. But I can't dream about that. We're not in a sunlit land here. Here it's a land of marshes, mists, and fogs. There's nothing I could do to change that, no matter how hard I dreamed. Even if I dreamed very, very hard. And I can't dream. At our place, we need rain and sunshine. My father always says so. It's for the crops, I understand. And also, if it didn't rain, the well would run dry. The marshes, too. So there would be nothing to drink. We would die, along with everyone else. It would be fine with me if everyone else died—but not us.

The rain stopped just as I got home. I leaned my bicycle against the wall of the barn and left it there. I leaned against the wall too, next to it, to catch my breath. I was tired, really tired. My bicycle would be safe enough.

I thought about that before I went into the house, because I'm very attached to my bicycle. It's the most precious thing I'll ever own, even if one day I become very rich. Even if I become very, very rich. It's simple. Without my bicycle I couldn't go to the high school. Obviously, there are buses that go to town, on Mondays and Saturdays. On Mondays, because of the boarders at the high school, and on Saturdays for the same reason and because of the market. The bus is expensive. I only come home every two weeks, except for this week, but this week is totally exceptional. I can't ask my parents, every two weeks, to pay for my bus trips. It's already a lot that they even agreed to let me go to the high school, I know. I don't ask for anything. Besides, if I asked, they wouldn't give me anything. That's how it is. As for the trip, I can do it by bike. I'm so happy to get to go to the high school that I pedal with incredible energy. On the downhills, I'm so happy that I sing at the top of my lungs.

Sometimes I'm tired and upset, like tonight. Not because of my bicycle and the twenty miles. Not at all. But it's dark as hell, and it really was raining very hard. I'll forget about it as soon as I go inside the house, with my mother and maybe all my sisters, who always make such a dreadful noise. In the past, when I didn't know that one day I'd be going to the high school, I couldn't stand all the noise. Now, it almost makes me happy. It's the sound of home.

I left my bike against the old wall of the barn for a number of reasons which guarantee that it will be totally safe. I'm certain of it. In winter, the house is so far from any walkable path, so far from any other house, behind the woods, the streams, and the wild waters of the marshes, that nobody's going to pass by here tonight. If anyone did, it would have to be a madman, and if it's a madman, my bicycle wouldn't be any safer in the courtyard in front of the house than against the wall of the barn. So.

Plus, nobody, that is, no one with any sense, would have any reason to want my bicycle. A thief who took it would only be throwing himself into the arms of the police, and in my village, everyone knows that thieves don't think it's at all funny to end up in the arms of the police. An ignorant thief from out of town might pass by, but on a night like this, that would be pretty astonishing. Except for the old Spaniard who lives with his goat, anybody would get swallowed up by the wild waters of the marshes before he could get here. And even if someone did get here, by some freak chance, and steal my bicycle, he'd soon be caught.

My bicycle, the most precious thing I will ever own, is also the most extraordinary object in our area. I don't know where it came from. I only know, because my father repeats this to me all the time, that it had a particularly glorious past, even if that was a long, long time ago, because my father got this information from his father.

In truth, the only original part of my bicycle that remains is its frame. The rust that's eating it up and piercing it through makes it clear that I'd better hurry up and finish my studies if I want it to carry me to school until the end. It has a frame with a crossbar that forces me to lean the bike to the side and lift my leg very high to straddle it. What remains of the seat is leather as hard and dry as stone, but I've wrapped it thickly in rags to make it harmless. The handlebars are remarkable for their grips, which are really high and allow me to sit up straight as I ride my bike. That's a great advantage. My back never hurts and I don't risk becoming hunchbacked like most of the girls at my high school. Let them laugh at me, I'm laughing at them. She who laughs last, laughs best. And if they are the last to laugh, as I suspect, they'll be laughing under the humps on their backs. That consoles me. Only a little. They're stupid and mean, the girls at my school. I hate them all. Except for Fanny.

My bicycle has skinny wheels with solid tires. I'm at no risk of getting a flat, I don't have to pump them up and re-pump them, like everyone else. I don't know if these are the original wheels, but my father says they're very rare, and that they must be treated with respect. He often says things like that, my father. At the back, I have a mudguard, but no rack. In front, I have neither a mudguard nor a headlamp. That's why I struggled so much in the dark, just now. The mudguard is very troublesome. The mud accumulates there and, after a while, my bike can't move anymore, and I have to either clean it off or carry it. The advantage is that nobody can steal it, and I can leave it against the wall of the barn without any fear. The mud around here is harder than cement.

I stayed quite a while, leaning against the wall, near my bicycle, thinking about all of this as I caught my breath. I needed to. I don't have a lot of breath. During the medical checkup at school, they told me I have a hypertrophied heart. That means too big. I thought that was funny. Usually it's less stressful when I return home. My mother comes to wait for me at the side of the road, at the corner by the woods. She brings a storm lamp so we can see where to put our feet, and avoid the ruts and holes of the marshes as much as possible. With my mother, I'm not afraid of the dark. Alone, I'm afraid, because I never know if it's dark because I've gone blind, or if it's dark because it's dark.

My mother helps me carry my bicycle through the water holes of the marshes. She never fails to come wait for me. She says I'm her favorite, that she would await my return for fifteen days and fifteen nights. She didn't want me to go to the high school, my mother. Not at all. She wanted me to stay near her always. I explained that I would come back soon, that I would earn a lot of money and that we would finally be able to buy good land, land without stones, where the wheat and the grapevines would grow up to the sky. Land far, far away from all these marshes. But she said no, that would be too late, it would take too long, she wanted me to stay near her. She wanted me to stay with her, and there would never be good land, never ever, unless I were there. Me, I went to the high school all the same. So now, my mother waits fifteen days and fifteen nights. Nobody can know. It's awful.

Tonight, my mother wasn't at the edge of the woods. She didn't know. I came back without warning. I wanted to bring back the things I'd taken from the high school. If they were found on me, I'd be expelled. I didn't have money to buy stamps and to write my mother to alert her to my arrival. Besides, it would have been useless. No letters ever come to our place.

At last I'd caught my breath. Time to go into the house. My troubles with my breath, my reflections and all of that were nothing more than ways to put off a little longer the moment when I would go inside. I've known myself for some time. I've often noticed: I'm excited to see someone, I hurry, I pedal my old bicycle for four hours, and I sing while crying from exhaustion in the rain. And then, when at last I get here, I don't know what to do. I do everything I can to put off the moment when I'll go back inside the house.

Because of all this, I'd wasted a fair amount of time. I had to go inside at last.

I took off the hood of my raincoat. It's a terrible hood. It has a cord that I can pull to gather the border, and then the hood envelops my head and leaves nothing exposed but my eyes and nose. When it's raining, when I'm on the bike, I appreciate its usefulness and its comfort. Only my nose gets wet. That's no big deal. You don't catch colds through your nose, my mother is firm on that subject. The only disadvantage of my raincoat, apart from its incredible ugliness, is that with my entire head wrapped tightly in that hood, I'm deaf. Though that's not really much of a disadvantage, it's true. Nobody ever calls for me, anywhere. And even if someone who wanted to pass me on the road called out, they wouldn't recognize me, disguised in this green thing that I use as a raincoat, which my uncle gave me when my aunt died. My aunt died this summer. I didn't tell Fanny where my raincoat came from. It would have horrified her and I don't want to do that. She's my friend and she's so beautiful. She hasn't asked me anything about my raincoat, which has helped me avoid lying. When people ask me questions, I often make up lies. I've gotten used to it, and it doesn't bother me anymore. But with Fanny, I would prefer to avoid lying. As for the raincoat, I figure she hasn't asked me about it because most people just assume that, if you have something, you simply bought it. Fanny can't know that with us it's almost never like that. Anyway, it's kept me from having to tell lies to Fanny.

I took my bag, which was tied to the handlebars of my bicycle. For once, it held no books, and was back to serving its original function. It's a black waxed canvas shopping bag. They're all over the place in the countryside, but you never see them at the high school. The girls have school satchels or proper travel bags. They laughed when they saw me with my old shopping bag. But it's fine with me if they laugh. I consider myself lucky to have it. Maman went to great difficulties to give it to me. I understand why. She used it a lot. With no trouble she can fit two pairs of chickens into it to take to the village and sell. For two months I begged her to let me have the bag. I believe she hoped, by refusing, to keep me from going to the high school and abandoning her. My mother came up with lots of tricks like that to keep me near her. I saw right through her. When she saw me making a bag from one of the jute sacks we use for wheat, which I'd taken from the hayloft, she gave up. She gave me her shopping bag. I flew into her arms and hugged her hard, telling her how much I loved her, how deeply I loved her, and always would. But she kept crying, she cried nonstop. She wouldn't stop crying. So I left her and went to dig potatoes as my father had told me to do, because they really had to be harvested.

Now, still, after the months I've spent in the company of this bag, I think of my mother every time I see it; and I always see it because I use it every day. So, on Thursday I stole a school satchel from Prisunic. It's easy at Prisunic. That way I would be able to give my mother back her shopping bag. I know very well that that's not what she was crying about.

I made up my mind to head toward the house. It was getting darker and darker, but I don't need to see to find my way to the house. At home, I can navigate with my eyes closed, I've gotten used to it. With Antonnella, my little sister, I do it all the time. I walk up the vine-edged path alongside the barn, I enter the yard in front of the house, paying attention to the pond that's right there, with its big pear tree that I used to climb in the past, when my father wanted to beat me. I'd climb so high that he couldn't reach me with his cattle prod, so high that, if he climbed up himself, the branches would be too weak to bear his weight. But my father never came after me when I was up in my pear tree. Though he climbed well, my father. I remember that, back in the days when he still hoped to buy good land without stones or marsh weeds, he'd climb the cherry tree, the one behind the house, whose branches are nearly all dead now. Because of the cold, my father says. At our place, the earth is cold. He would pick the ripe cherries from the branches that reached highest to the sky and throw them down to us on the ground. We were happy as could be. We made ourselves earrings with the cherries to make them last longer. We would end up eating them. Or else, one of us would take some cherries from another of us, and we'd all start shouting and fighting, and my father would come with a stick and beat one of us girls, it didn't matter which, usually it was me, because with so many girls, he couldn't be sure which one to beat. It wasn't very important. The victim would seek revenge on her own. Anyway, in the end he stopped interfering in our business. I mean, what else could he do, with so many daughters being born year after year, who wouldn't stop coming.

I didn't tell Fanny how many girls there are at home. My father thinks it's a curse. I told Fanny, "All my sisters are dead. One summer evening while they were sitting by the fire, a storm came, lightning struck, and all my sisters died." I thought it was a good story. It's a lie, obviously. But it could have been the truth. The night the lightning struck, my sisters were singing in a circle around the fireplace. My father, my mother, and I were working in the barn. A cow was calving, and was having a lot of trouble because it was the first time this had happened to her. We had to help her. That's normal. I told everything in detail to Fanny. And it's true that I've often helped birth the little calves. Sometimes they're born in the meadows, and I have to look after the cow if she needs me. By necessity, I've had to get used to it. I get by very well. I even prefer helping the cows to helping my mother. It's prettier to see. All the cows are happy with their little ones. They don't ask questions afterwards, they lick them gently, for a long time. It's pretty. My mother, when she has little ones, screams because it hurts. Afterwards, she cries because it's a daughter again, and she doesn't want more daughters. I understand, of course. But the baby can't do anything about that. My mother refuses to feed it, and me, I have to take care of it and everything if I don't want it to die. The baby is happy. It doesn't know yet that it's a girl and that it will regret it.

But this I didn't tell Fanny. I only told her the story of the cow's first little calf, which we gently pulled out by its front hooves to help it leave its mother's belly. When you're in the middle of doing that, you can't think of anything else, so much so that we didn't even hear the storm arrive.

When we went back into the house, we saw all my sisters silent and motionless, their mouths open in song. We buried them all together in a box made from the wood of a poplar my father chopped down for the purpose. Now, on windy nights, when there has been a lot of sun, and the strong fragrance of syringas and flowering vines fills the countryside, you still can hear my dead sisters singing. Fanny said that one day she'd come to my place to hear it. Me, I said nothing in response, because all that, it's lies. It could have been true but it's not true. Besides, I don't want Fanny to come to our house. Ever. I don't want to go to her house either, on the Sundays when I stay at the high school and she invites me over. Her place and my place, it's not the same thing. I don't want her to know how we live at home. And I don't want to go to her place because of my clothes. My clothes are so pathetic that people laugh when they see me. So I will never go.

I advanced along the path with my bag that weighed on my arm, whose straps cut into my hand. It had lost its handles and I'd replaced them with string. In the path, the mud stuck to my boots so terribly that I wondered for a moment if the pond had overflowed. That can happen in winter. I remember even more astonishing floods. For instance, once, a long time ago, I was still little, it had rained heavily for days and days. A rain to end the world, for days and days. And one afternoon we were all in the kitchen making a lot of noise as usual, talking about nothing, arguing, fighting, in short, the usual. All of a sudden, we heard an extraordinary boom, as if a plane had shaved off the top of the house. The dog began to howl and we all ran outside, silent for once, we were so impressed. Then we saw a sort of enormous lake of water moving at top speed, carrying away with it everything in its path. It was truly the most impressive thing we had ever seen. The lake passed just to the side of the house and went on to rejoin the streams and the marshes. What happened after that, I don't know.

If it had touched our house it certainly would have carried it away, and us with it, and the cows, the dog, the fowl, my mother's two pigs, in short, everything. Really it would have been a strange journey. Thinking about it moved us so much that we kept quiet the whole rest of the day. And it's true that when even the water stops following a normal course, nobody knows what to do.

The pond hadn't overflowed, and that made me happy. I wouldn't like to die of drowning. That must be an unbearable way to die.

I entered the yard. The shutters of the house were closed, but a little light filtered out through the slats. Everything was silent. My sisters must have been sleeping, even that great big pest Maria. I know the habits of the house well. I could picture my mother by the fire. She would be knitting, or maybe reading one of Aunt Gina's romance novels, or maybe thinking of me. When she thinks of me, she cries as if I were dead. As for my father, either he was sleeping, or he was tinkering with one of the gadgets he'd made, which save him a lot of money because he does everything himself, which is necessary if he's ever going to buy good land and make a living. My father invents a lot of these gadgets—he dreams them up on his own. My mother says he has talent as an inventor. It's true. No doubt that's what was going on in the kitchen. And the day must have been a reasonably good one since my father and my mother weren't arguing. I was happy about that. They often argue, my father and mother. That's normal. Sometimes they fight. I can't stand that.

I thought of the moment when I would open the door. Maman would rush out shouting *Galla!* and crying. She'd clasp me very hard in her arms, begging me never to go away from her again. Never again, Galla. Never again.

Every time, it's like that. Always like that. Every time. I don't want to get there, ever.

I longed to return for a moment to the old wall of the barn and to stay there quietly. I could do that because everything seemed normal at home. From seeing my mother cry, I'd become afraid of all the terrifying things that might happen while I was away. For example, the house and the barn on fire, the animals burnt to ashes or falling into unsuspected holes in the marshes. Sometimes, at the high school, fears like that took such hold of me that I actually expected a phone call informing me of the dire news. Whenever I come back home and find out that everything is in order, I could leap for joy, leap with intense joy, and leave straightaway. Because, on the Sundays when I'm home, Maman cries from morning until night, and the crying gradually increases as she realizes that I'm going to leave again all the same. I love my mother. Nobody loves her more than I do. But everything is unbearable. Unbearable. So, last Sunday, all of a sudden, I felts overwhelmed, so desperate with this sorrow, these entreaties, threats, everything, and that she was going to die, finally, everything, really everything, I was so beside myself that I shouted, "I wish you weren't my mother! That you weren't my mother!"

I didn't mean it. I swear on my honor I didn't mean it at all. And on Antonnella's honor. But it's just that I couldn't take it anymore, I want to go to the high school, I couldn't take it anymore.

I was sorry for having said that. All week long I felt more afraid than usual. So I took a school satchel from Prisunic and some things from the high school, and tonight I came back to see how things were. My mother will understand that I love her, that I didn't mean what I said at all, about wishing she wasn't my mother. She knows it, but I have to tell her. Me, I would love for anyone to say that to me, except for my mother.

I wasn't very eager to go into the house. I stayed there, telling myself sad and completely idiotic things. That's the way I am. I tell myself silly things completely seriously, as if they made sense. That's how I get when I have no desire to do something I've got to do. Stuck in place, telling myself stories about nothing.

I told myself, to buy time, that I could go pay a visit to Daisy. Daisy is my dog. She sleeps in the barn's utility shed, in a nest of straw. She has a puppy right now. We haven't given it a name because we aren't going to keep it. I think it's for Aunt Gina. I hate her like I hate all my aunts, she's a hyena, but she doesn't mistreat animals. We can give her Daisy's puppy. He's as funny as can be. His belly is so heavy that it drags on the ground, and to move about, the puppy paddles with his little paws at the side. He looks like a fat tadpole. He's really very funny and I can't keep from laughing and loving him. His mother loves him too. When she sees him move away, she runs after him. Early on, she would take his head in her jaws to carry him back to the bed. Now that he's too fat, she pulls him by his tail and he whimpers and protests. She's a good mother, she's afraid he'll hurt himself. Afterwards, she licks him, for a long time. She's really a very good mother, Daisy.

2

I HEADED toward Daisy's straw bed. I called out *Daisy!*

At once, there was a great commotion in the straw and Daisy was there, leaping everywhere and whining with joy. She didn't even bark, or hesitate. She knew at once that it was me. She knows me too well to make a mistake. I've spent more days of my life with her than with any other member of my family. We watch the cows together and I always take her everywhere with me. We're very close friends. She, too, feels great sorrow that I've gone off to high school... She doesn't show it, but I can tell from the crazy joy she displays when I come back. When I leave, she doesn't whine or bark, or anything. She knows very well that I'm sad, too, she's intelligent. I could tell loads of stories about her, and I tell them to Fanny because she understands everything, Fanny.

Whenever I arrive at her side, Daisy whines and jumps with frenzied joy. I crouch down, she rests her soft head on my shoulder and her cold nose trembles against my neck. That's her way of hugging me. We stay there a while, that way, quietly loving each other. Afterwards I get back up. At that moment, if she has a little one, she looks at me, muzzle raised, wags her fluffy tail and heads towards her bed. She wants to introduce her son or daughter to me. When I've properly admired and petted her marvel of a puppy, she heads toward the house, like the mistress of the manor, to invite me to enter. Me, I follow her, of course.

Normally, after I've seen how much her little one has plumped up and grown, I wait for Daisy to lead me to the house. But she stayed put. At last I said to her, "Are you coming, Daisy?" But she didn't move. I said, "What's wrong?

She whimpered a little but didn't move. So, I decided she had to have reasons of her own for keeping close by her puppy. She does that when she senses that we're about to take it away from her and give it to strangers. She refuses to leave her bed. I thought about that a little and then decided to go into the house alone. In any case, it would be a nice surprise for my mother.

I left Daisy and walked towards the door of the house. There I was very surprised because Daisy took one leap to get to the door of the house and started barking very loudly, in a weird way, the way she does when she bares her teeth and fights with other dogs. I said, "Shut up, Daisy!"

Normally, I never tell Daisy to shut up. If she barks, she has her reasons. But this time, I couldn't stop myself because it really amazed me. She didn't shut up, on the contrary. She came toward me full of joy, then made for the door of the house again, barking and whimpering.

I began to be a little afraid she'd gone mad. That happens sometimes. When it does, it seems nothing can be done. You've got to put down a dog that has become a danger even to those it loves. If Daisy went mad and had to be killed, it would be terrible. Terrible. My father kills dogs by hanging them. That's how he is, my father. It's horrible, a hanged dog.

I didn't have time to think these things through. All of a sudden, the door of the kitchen opened. I wasn't expecting that. Not at all. There was no time to run away. I should have run away.

Obviously, it was natural that someone would come out to see what was going on, what with the noise Daisy was making and the bizarre way she was barking. Only, in my head, throughout the entire return journey, I'd pictured things differently. I was going to be the one who opened the door. This changed everything. Me, I'd imagined that, suddenly, as my father and mother waited quietly by the fire, I would come in, I'd run to my mother who would be stupefied with joy, and I'd say, as I threw myself into her arms, "It's me, Maman! I came back to see you."

Then she would understand everything I meant to say, that I love her more than anything, even though I've gone far away from her. Failing that, she'd come out and say, "Galla! My Galla! Here you are at last. My daughter."... Finally. That would completely change everything. When my mother says things like that to me, and she says them incessantly, I feel carried away with sadness and fury, I don't know why, that's how I am.

Since everything had changed, I didn't move. I waited with Daisy, who howled like mad. A true fool.

The door remained open and for a long while, nothing appeared but a big rectangle of light. This lasted so long that I began to hope my mother would finally show up and everything would be over. And then a silhouette emerged from the light, without a word. I didn't recognize it right away because I could tell that it wasn't my mother. The dog whined and leapt around me. Then my father said, "Enough, Daisy!"

Daisy whined more quietly. My father said, "What is it?"

I said, "It's me. Galla."

He said, "You?"

How strange his voice sounded. But in the dark, everything can seem unusual. I waited for him to get out of the doorway so I could go inside. I was so cold. But he stayed there, planted, saying nothing, and it was like I was a stranger and he had to think it over before deciding whether or not to let me into the house. Maybe it was because of the whining of that blasted Daisy. I felt full of fury, all at once, and I gave her a sharp kick to calm her down, saying, "Shut up, already!"

She yelped and ran off toward the barn. I shouldn't have done that. But I was so sad about all of this.

Then my father said, "Get out of here!"

I stayed in place, numb. He wouldn't chase me away for kicking the dog. Him, he gives her terrible kicks when she misbehaves or when he's angry. I kept waiting without moving, thinking that his anger would soon pass. Then he said it again, "Get out of here!"

He went back inside and locked the door.

3

I STAYED there a while, standing amid the mud and the puddles of the yard. I didn't know what to do anymore. I was so tired out from everything, and the night was so dark. All at once, I was reminded of old Midsummer's Eve festivals, nights with skies full of stars and the earth lit by bonfires. Ancient, illuminated evenings that we watched for ages, motionless, my little sisters and me.

At our place, we don't make a bonfire on Midsummer's Eve. My father doesn't want to. I don't know why. If we ask him, he doesn't answer. That's how he is. Sometimes I think my parents are crazy. Sometimes I tell myself it would be better if I didn't have parents, not anywhere in the world, and if no parent had me for a daughter. Because, when I think about it coldly, I have to admit that I wouldn't like to be my mother. Not at all. I'm not mean-spirited at all, at least, I don't think I am. All the same, I wouldn't like to have me for a daughter, not at all. And I understand perfectly well that nobody wanted me when I was born. I too would have preferred not to be born. It's so sad: my whole life, and being me. It's so sad that I would have preferred not to be born, and for everyone to be happy. I can't say I resent my parents, or myself, no. I was born so long ago now that I've had time to get used to it. And besides, many people are born like that, by bad luck. I think that if there was no one on the planet but people who'd been wanted, the planet would be almost deserted. I don't know. Often I amuse myself by thinking how that would be. I can't picture the house deserted and the earth inhabited by a profusion of flowers, stars, and bonfires, on those long-ago Midsummer's Eve nights. I wouldn't have been there. All the same, how I would have loved to live on an earth like that one, with only people who'd been wanted. All the people would be beautiful, like Fanny, who is full of sunshine and so lovely to look at.

What I would like is for it to start raining and raining, and for the rain to drown all the unwanted.

At the high school, I read that in certain countries they get rid of people that nobody wants. I read that, once, in China, you could kill little girls if you didn't want them. I think that's good. It's sad to drown a baby, or a dog, or a cat. But it's good too. That way there aren't more unwanted. In Brazil it's the same thing, with beggars. If I'd been born in Brazil, maybe one day they'd have loaded me onto a boat and shipped me far out into the middle of the ocean, very far, and drowned me. Later, they would have found my body purple and swollen with water on a beach. I've never seen a beach. Never. What I would like to know is what the people who warm themselves in the sun of beaches would have done with me. Would they have thrown me back into the ocean or let me rot there in the sun on the beach? I don't know. Maybe they would have taken me and put me into the ground. It would make me sad to rot in the sun, on the soft sand of beaches. But once I'm dead, perhaps it will be all the same to me. Completely the same. You can't know in advance what you'll think when you're dead.

What would really make me happy would be to die in the hot deserts of Australia, someplace where nobody could see me. They say that, after a very long time, explorers find little bits of bone, fragile, smooth, and bleached by the sun. They have no idea anymore who they belonged to when they were still living. That's what I would like. To me this seems pretty and clean. And nobody would know anything anymore.

But for this to happen, I would have to have been born in Australia, or to have a lot of money so I could go there. But I only have my bicycle, already so old and worn-out; and later, if I have any money, it will go to buy good land where we can make a living. It's always like that. I can't decide how I'm to live or how I'm to die. As for living, it doesn't matter much to me, now that I'm grown. You get used to everything. But when it comes to dying, that's sadder, because nobody wants to die, and when you die, you die for always. You should at least be able to choose. When it seems to me that it's unbearable to be alive, I tell myself that tomorrow or later on, it will be different. Even if I know it's not true, I believe it a little. But when you die, you know very well that it's for always.

All of that is unfair and I think about it often. I wish everything were fair and happy. And then I come home, struggling all alone in the rain and singing in the dark, and my father says to me, "Get out of here!" Me, I don't know where to go.

I went to the storage shed in the barn to sit by Daisy and think a little. Daisy's always happy when you go to her. You're always welcome, it's not like with people. I pet Daisy, who has stretched her head across my lap, and we stay like that for a while. I was fine. I spoke to her gently, to be forgiven for the kick. But I don't think she resented me for it at all. She's a smart dog who understands life. I petted her for a long time, and ran my fingers through her long, coarse hair.

I recalled some things Fanny told me one day. It was a long time ago. We weren't friends yet. It was when I told her I was born on St. Pepin's Day. I think it's funny to have been born on that day. When I told Fanny about it, she laughed, she didn't believe me. I convinced her, since it's true. Before, I had said to her, "Did your parents want you, when you were born?"

She looked at me. We didn't know each other well. We didn't know we would become friends. She said, "Yes. Of course." Later, she said, "Why?"

And I said, "Me, nobody wanted me. And then, to really put them out, I arrived on St. Pepin's Day."

She laughed. She's very beautiful when she laughs, Fanny. She thought I was just trying to be witty. I said, "You are beautiful because your parents wanted you. That's why."

She said, "You're beautiful, too. Only, you always have such a sad face. But when you laugh, your eyes are full of stars."

I said nothing. It isn't true, of course. But now, when I think of Fanny, I remember that she said that. It makes me happy, even if it's not true.

Daisy had fallen asleep, her head on my lap, her puppy in the hollow of her stomach. I couldn't even hear her breathing. Dogs and children make no noise when they sleep and are pretty to look at. I petted Daisy's head, which moved a little. I took advantage of that to get up.

It was terribly cold. I hate the cold even more than all those mists on the marshes around the house. Truly, I hate all of that. I wish so much I had been born in a land of sunshine.

I asked myself what I was going to do. The light was still on in the kitchen. My father must have been finishing up some job he'd started. That's how he is. He only likes finished work. My mother says that's a great quality. It must be true. But there are days when qualities become flaws. Which is why I would have to go on waiting to enter the house. Luckily, I'm used to that. My father often throws me out. Every time he's angry—and he's often angry, because of this life we lead, this land filled with white stones, all these daughters and never any money for anything. I understand all that. Also, when he throws me out, at first I'm furious, afterwards, I think about it, and I'm not angry at all. The only thing I regret is that he never throws out that great big pest Maria. Not even once. But as long as it's never her, I'd rather it be me instead of one of the little ones. It's really very sad to be all alone in the dark outside, even if you understand.

Sometimes, my father is right to throw me out. I remember one time especially. I was still little. Eight or nine. We had killed the pig. The man who kills all the pigs in the area, a kind of professional hog butcher, was at the house. They didn't send me to school the day they slaughtered the pig. I could be useful. My father had given me the task of cutting meat into pieces. In a while, I don't know how it happened, the knife cut my thumb, a big chunk of flesh. It was disgusting—blood flowing all over, and the chunk of flesh dangling. My father noticed it. I'd never seen him so angry. He didn't even have to open the door, it was already open. All I remember is an enormous kick and afterwards I was on the ground, in the mud, in the middle of the courtyard. On the way, I lost the chunk that dangled from my thumb. Now I have a very ugly thumb, with a big gouge out of it.

After that, I felt so humiliated that my father would have beaten me in front of that strange man that I decided to go a long way away from home and never come back. I thought I would live like the little girl in *En Famille*, cooking for myself in old tin cans and all the rest, exactly like her. I had just read the book. So I left, very determined. Along the way, I turned back several times, looking back at the house. I was happy to be going far away, to be living on my own, to never be at home anymore. I said, "Adieu, disgusting house! I will never see you again!"

I felt sure I would leave. I walked quite a while in the dark. Arriving at the marshes, I began to feel very afraid. The fog is always so thick there, and back then, I was still little, I didn't know the marshes well. Worst of all is that I started thinking about the old Spaniard who lives all alone with his goat, wandering these lands of wild waters and fog. Running like a fool, I retraced my steps. Afterwards, I forgot that I'd wanted to leave. Every time I wanted to leave there was always night and fog like that. So I could never leave.

The light was still burning in the kitchen. In winter, my father goes to bed late. He hasn't been tired out by working in the fields. I wondered if my mother was thinking of coming to open the door for me. Ordinarily, she comes. She says nothing when my father beats me and throws me out, but then she comes and opens the door for me. I don't hold that against her, of course. If she interfered, my father would beat her, and I don't want that. I can't bear it. It makes me practically crazy. When I was little and those things happened so often, I wished that one night my father would go away and never come back. Not that he would die, no. Simply, one day he would go to town on business, and then, at night we would wait for him and he wouldn't come back. He always came back. But me, I often dreamed of a home without shouting, without fear, a quiet home.

Whenever my father throws me out before dinner, my mother comes and brings me a little something to eat. She pretends she has something to do, the henhouses to close, a forgotten brood of chicks, anything, no matter what, and she comes out to be with me for a moment. She tells me about her life and everything. Sometimes Maria figures out what Maman has in mind. Maria is the nastiest pest on earth. She alerts my father. My father says nothing and Maria is stuck . . . My father never hears when you talk to him. Nobody knows what he's thinking, not even my mother. What's sure is that he never hears what we say to him and he never responds.

When everyone has gone to bed and fallen asleep, my mother gets up softly and comes to open the door. In winter, if I'm very cold, she makes me mulled wine with cinnamon to warm me. I love the smell of cinnamon. And my mother tells me stories and tells me she loves me, that I'm her favorite, and how much I look like her.

I hoped very hard that my father would go to bed soon. I have a lot of patience, through force of habit. But it was really cold out. Very, very cold.

To pass the time, I decided to circle the house and see if it looked like everyone was sleeping.

The shutters of my mother's bedroom were closed. They always are, even in the daytime. Nobody opens them. Light filters in through two crooked slats, and while she waits for my father, my mother reads her romance novels. She loves romance novels. That obnoxious Aunt Gina lends them to her because she loves them too, which is surprising because Aunt Gina is so gaunt and forever dressed in black. She's an appalling sight. All my aunts are like that, and I happen to have a lot of them. Seeing them all together, you'd think they were an army of candles in mourning. Even the dogs pick up on it. I remember a summer day when all of them came to our house together. It was for a burial. When he saw them, the dog didn't bark or anything. He threw himself at the front door, and raising his head skyward, his paws stiffly spread, he began howling his head off. He howled nonstop, straining towards the white sky, icy breaths cutting the heavy air. Nobody dared speak. My black aunts stayed there, motionless, amid the silence, the fear, and that barking, facing the crazy dog who was howling his head off.

That's how they are, my aunts.

I thought my mother must surely be reading her romance novels, and after a while, I contented myself with that thought. She wouldn't go to sleep, she'd come and open the door for me as soon as she could. It was so dark and so sad. I kept on circling the house. And all at once, amid this silence and this darkness, it felt so odd to be there, circling the house, that I felt like a stranger or a lost animal searching for some hole through which to slip into the house, or a stray animal, circling the house with such patience, circling and circling, hoping to see the doors open.

I asked myself if other unknown people had ever circled the house silently like I was doing. There are so many marshes, streams to cross, sullen waters tangled with tough grasses, through which the old Spaniard endlessly wanders. Nobody can escape.

The shutters of the girls' bedroom were closed too. No noise came from them. All of them were sleeping. For my sisters, it's a matter of complete indifference whether I'm there or not. They didn't know I was there, in front of their window. But if they had known, it wouldn't have mattered to them. They wouldn't even have let me in. That's how it is at home, I'm used to it. Only little Antonnella would have been delighted. She's three years old. I'm the one who named her, Antonnella. In our house, nobody bothers to think up names when a baby is going to be born. A first name, I think that's important. The only one they ever looked for was for a boy. Aimé. Now we all know there won't be a boy, and though we're used to that, we still don't talk about it the way we once did. And Maman is going to have another baby in a few months.

Antonnella was very sad that I was going to the high school. I always paid a lot of attention to her. Maman, when she was expecting her, was convinced she was going to die in childbirth. My mother always thinks she's going to die bringing us into the world. It's almost a mania. She should have gotten used to it by now. With Antonnella, she thought about her own death even more than with all the others. She talked to me about it endlessly, crying about having to die that way, and abandoning us. She cried and told me she entrusted me with the baby and the other sisters, and her two pigs, the chickens, the pâté ducks, essentially everything. She talked about it so much that in the end I also was certain she would die. And then Antonnella was born; so timid, so minuscule, she couldn't hurt a fly. She's so pretty! But I had a lot of trouble with her. She couldn't tolerate milk, and I didn't know what to do. In the end, I fed her milk mixed with broth. Now she's still tiny, but livelier. She wants to go everywhere with me, and when she talks to me her big eyes, blue as wild chicory flowers, open wide, and truly you would think that she sees me. Since I've been going to the high school, she's been sad, she's wasting away. She doesn't cry or complain or anything. But her pale little face is becoming transparent. Poor little Antonnella. I know what's wrong with her. She thought she was part of me, and now that I've gone away without her, she realizes she isn't. That's not something you ever get over. I know this because I was like that for a long time with my mother. I thought I was her. It's funny to think about and even a little disgusting. I can't recall the time when I thought I was part of Maman, but I remember the day when I understood that she and I were two distinct people, and after that the world was never the same. Never again.

It was one of those luminous summer days. My mother was selling two baskets of peaches in the village. From the moment she left the house, I began waiting for her. When Maman wasn't there, I wasn't even alive. The house was so sad, so sad, and it seemed to me she would never be coming back home. She said she would leave one day and abandon us all. So I believed that she would never return from the village. I would wait for her for a very long time, but she wouldn't come back. That day, I couldn't wait any longer.

I went to meet her by the edge of the marshes. I was sitting on the ground, facing the crazy clusters of yellow irises, and running my fingers through the damp earth, which was fun in a small way. I didn't dare go farther, I didn't know the way out. So I stayed there all alone, looking at the wild, waterlogged land with its solitary rivulets where taciturn plants grew. I don't know what happened, or why. I only know that, all of a sudden, I understood that Maman and I were separate. Two people who were completely distinct, forever. An unbearable sorrow gripped me. A sorrow as great as all the loneliness of the earth. From that day on, I could see *me*. Now that I'm grown, it hardly matters. But that day, I saw *me*, so small, hardly visible next to all those water-crazed flowers, and Maman so far away, separated from me for always.

So I feel very sorry for Antonnella, Antonnella, she's such a fragile little flower, and I...what can I do to make her stop feeling bad? I feel so bad.

There I was, thinking about those sad things, leaning against the closed outside shutters, when all at once I really wanted to see Antonnella. I knocked on the shutters, softly so nobody else could hear and so she wouldn't be afraid. Inside, nothing moved. Maybe my mother had taken my little sister into her bed. That happens often, now. I was sorry. I would have liked to tell her I was there, so near to her, that I was going to come and sleep, holding her to me the way she likes, cuddled up into a hot little ball in my arms.

I wondered if anyone had read her the story of *The Three Little Pigs* that night. I took that book from Prisunic, the first Thursday of the fall. It has pretty pictures. She was so full of joy, Antonnella. Since then, every night when I'm home she sits on my lap and asks me to read the story to her. At these times, she pretends to look at the pictures or the outlines as if she could see. At the moment when the unlucky little pigs are devoured by the wolf, I pretend to weep over the dead little pigs. Then Antonnella puts her arms around my neck, soothes me, and shows me the cover of the book where she knows there's a picture of the three little pigs. She says, "Don't cry! They aren't dead, they're all there."

And it's true. We're as happy as can be, the two of us. I would like to know if anyone ever reads the story to her when I'm not there. She's so cute, Antonnella—it's almost dreadful to think of her.

I went halfway around. I stopped again under the window of my mother's bedroom. I called out quietly, pressing my mouth to the crack between the two crooked slats. Then I called again several times, more loudly. She didn't answer. She must have fallen asleep over her romance novels. She often rereads the same ones. Evidently, they're so boring that she falls asleep over them. Oh well. All of a sudden I felt so sad. She was sleeping there, so close, but I couldn't see her or put my arms around her. I didn't even want to see her and put my arms around her. I just wanted her to know I was there, in the dark, under the window, looking through this crack of light. I thought maybe my mother didn't love me as much as she said, since she couldn't hear me calling, since she was sleeping while I was waiting outdoors.

Immediately, I started reproaching myself for having such thoughts. But it was so cold everywhere outside the locked house and my father didn't want me to come in. These sorts of suspicions come to me whenever things seem more unbearable than usual. At night everything is unbearable. And also, I love my mother and I told her I wished she wasn't my mother. I do everything I can for her. I'm not only talking about housework. That's fair enough, or at least, it would be if everyone worked, in particular that nasty, lazy pest Maria, who thinks she's the Holy Sacrament because she's beautiful, and it's true she's beautiful, but that's no reason. I'm talking about other things, like letting myself get beaten in Maman's place when she does silly things, breaks dishes or the big black umbrella, or loses the keys or something else, and I tell my father it was me. And also, when I come back home to help her with everything, every night, even the day of the village festival. We all go there, to the festival, Maria far ahead with her girlfriends, me and the little ones behind. Maria and her girlfriends laugh like hyenas, looking at boys who are even more idiotic than they are. Maria never wants me with her. She says she's ashamed of me. I get it. Me too, I'm ashamed of being so badly dressed and dark as a gypsy, as my father says. Only, in the village, everyone knows I'm her sister anyway, even if she tries to go where I'm not. It must be unbearable for her to have me for a sister and not to be able to do anything about it. For me, of course, the festival's no big deal. The more I listen to the music and the more I watch the others, the more I understand that nobody will want me. So I start thinking about my mother all alone at home. Everything that could happen to her. My father will take advantage of our absence to beat her. In short, sad things. I leave the little ones at the festival and I go back home, running the whole way. At home, nothing has happened to Maman. She reads her novels on Sundays. I throw my arms around her and tell her how much I love her forever and ever.

And it's true. It's also true that I wish she weren't my mother. I could have gone to the high school in peace, without abandoning anyone, and someday later, leave home without looking back. That's what I dream. But I can't.

I left the window and went to the barn, taking care to keep my feet out of the muddy water so I wouldn't make noise. My father didn't seem in any hurry to go to bed. He didn't come out into the dark and cold. I wondered what to do while I waited, and then I decided to stay with Daisy again. I went near and called her. She woke up at once and came to me wriggling with frenzied joy. I said to her, "Make room for me, Daisy."

She waited until I was well settled in her bed with the puppy and then she stretched herself out against me. She's always gentle and warm, Daisy. I was fine.

4

I GOT UP abruptly, jolts of pain shooting through my body.
It took me a while to understand where I was. It was the first
time in my life that I'd slept in the straw with the dog. I
wasn't used to that. Of course, I'd slept in the straw before,
at my godmother's house, in summertime, when my mother
sent me there to work, because that way I got meals for free.
But there the straw had been laid out in a corner of the
granary especially for me. It wasn't the same thing at all.
This time I was in the shed, in the straw with the dog. I
wasn't at all used to that.

I heard Daisy's barking, coming from behind the barn.
She must have been gone a long time, because I was very cold.
I was irritated, even though I knew very well that Daisy's job
was to watch the house, not to keep me warm. Still, nobody
was threatening the house or my bicycle. Daisy probably had
to do her business, as was natural, and because she's very
clean, she goes far off in the fields to relieve herself, then she
barks a little for form. She's not at all like the town dogs. In
town, the sidewalks on the streets that lead to the high school
are covered in dog droppings. It's completely disgusting. This
when there are gutters with flowing water. But no. People
let their dogs relieve themselves on the sidewalks, or against
car tires. Clean, rich people; and yet, in the streets that belong
to everybody, they behave disgustingly. When I see that, I

tell myself that people wouldn't dare to drop their drawers there and do what they have their dogs do. Then I tell myself, too, that all those clean people are more disgusted by themselves than by their dogs, and that—that's really terrible. Anyway, the richest neighborhoods have the dirtiest sidewalks because of the great number of dogs. You could even identify those neighborhoods by their dirty sidewalks, without taking the houses into consideration. It makes me laugh to think about it. But in reality, it's pretty troubling. Because even the yard of our house, with all the animals and us girls, who are all very dirty, isn't as repulsive as these sidewalks of the rich. Still, we can't take the cows someplace far away to do their business. A cow isn't a dog. Truly, these town people are filthy creatures. Nothing less. You can tell because of their dogs. To them it doesn't matter. They imagine that they and their dogs are not the same thing. But it's just the same.

I would have liked to know what time it was. I don't have a watch. Like everyone else, I had my First Communion, but even so, I don't have a watch. My godmother didn't give me one, or anything else, for that matter. At home, only Maria has one. She has a nice godmother. She died this summer. She was also my aunt, because each of us has an aunt for a godmother. That might be fun if my aunts hadn't all been dressed in black ever since I'd known them, and if they didn't give a person the impression of being accompanied by black ghosts. I think it's very sad to have been baptized that way. My mother says it couldn't have been any other way, that all our aunts are like that, and there's nothing to be done, and that's true. Now we only have a few aunts left for any little ones still at risk of being born, I know my mother. If too many are born, I don't know how we'll find godmothers. Really, it makes no difference, since our godmothers never give us anything. Except, of course, for that great big pest Maria, but hers died this summer. It serves her right, Maria.

I got up gently to avoid waking Daisy's puppy. The kitchen light wasn't on anymore. My mother must have opened the door, looked for me, maybe. And me, I was asleep. I'm unforgivable. Totally unforgivable. I felt again how much I hated myself. It was very cold.

I tried to open the door of the house. It was locked. I tried again many times, to double-check. No doubt about it: the door was locked. This puzzled me. I hadn't expected this at all. My mother had never left me shut outside the house. The only possible explanation was that my mother didn't know I'd come back. She and my father never talk about me.

All at once, I began to get angry. Enormously angry, uncontrollably angry, as I'd never been before. Because nobody has the right to treat her daughter that way, however bad she is. Even animals love their offspring and take care of them. And me? What had I done to make nobody want me? I wanted, all of a sudden, to rise up all alone against the world and demand at last: What had I done, that nobody wanted me?

There I was, filled with that terrible energy, when Daisy came up to me. I wasn't thinking about her anymore at all. She panted in the dark, her muzzle pressed against me, all happy that I was there. I petted her narrow foxy head and she shook herself. I said to her, "Blast it Daisy, go away!" because I was lucky enough to have her. Surely there are people in the world who don't even have a dog or a goat they can calmly go to sleep with.

I went back to Daisy's bed and she followed me. What confidence she has! The puppy was still asleep. It's such a tender thing, a sleeping puppy, like a baby. I took it in my arms and settled myself in the bed. Daisy arranged herself against me. She understands everything. I put the puppy in the hollow of her belly. They fell asleep almost at once. In sum, if I'd been a puppy I would have been loved. Daisy spends her time looking out for her little one, licking him, letting him nurse even when he hurts her with his sharp little teeth. And me, I've always been deprived of everything. Me, I've never been able to love anything, because nobody wanted me. I know that my mother didn't have time to look after me, what with the field work, the livestock, my father, Maria and the other babies that never stopped coming, and after that, Aunt Gina's romance novels. I don't miss the caresses I never had. They horrify me. Even right now, if someone brought a damp mouth to me for a kiss I would slap them hard, I'd be so horrified. Except for my mother. She's my mother. And Fanny. She has smooth, freckled cheeks, like warm bread. She's so pretty. Fanny, you could never imagine slapping her. If I'd been loved, I'd be pretty, too. It would have been enough for me to be a puppy or any kind of domestic animal. My father and mother take good care of animals. As for me, when I was little, I would have liked to be a little calf. I would have been loved, like everybody.

I was hot; I wanted to move, but didn't dare, afraid of waking the dog, who might go off again to the stream and the marshes to bark at the wind and the moon, and the birds that call in the night. I tried not to move, but it was hard. Because I knew that I must not move, I felt like I absolutely had to, and the feeling was so strong that it made my legs and everything else ache. That's how I am.

I tried to distract myself by thinking of other things, as I often do. I tried to come up with a topic of conversation as if I were two people, though I had to be extra careful since for the most part the things I talk to myself about are sad things. The only happy thought in my life is Fanny, and all that sunshine she carries inside herself. But when I think of her, there's nothing to say except that I'm so happy, and I'm longing to see her. It's sad. She's so marvelous, Fanny, so beautiful, that she likes everyone, even long-legged Lydia. Me, I don't like anyone. When I think of Lydia, her wickedness makes me angry, or her ugliness makes me sad, and I wonder: Do her parents love her, ugly and wicked as she is? Fanny says yes, that parents are parents. Me, I don't believe it. They must see her giant crowded teeth and her lashless eyelids. And then, even if her parents do love her, no man ever will. It's terrible, really. Because she makes so many plans. When she's going to get married, what kind of house she'll have, the kids, the friends, all of that. Me, I tell myself that her life is not going to turn out like that, and that it's not fair to be so ugly that nothing is possible.

This morning, she started in again with that nonsense about the water lilies. I hate her. The English professor, too. He talks to us endlessly about people who've been dead forever, instead of leaving them in peace, which they definitely deserve, or telling stories of his own. I can't bear the whole business anymore. If only he spoke in English, then we wouldn't understand. But no. Everything he tells us is in French. He's completely insane.

This morning he told the story of a girl named Ophelia, an old story. It interested me all the same because of my cousin Ophélie, my Aunt Gina's daughter, who's a kind of candle like her mother, but even yellower, serious and as stiff as the devil. I'd like to know what kind of life you can expect to live with a name like Ophelia.

In the professor's story, Ophelia doesn't look like my cousin at all. She's a beautiful young girl with long blond hair, sweet and fair as a water nymph. She's very in love with a boy, Hamlet, and he's very in love with her, too. It started well. They could have been happy if the boy hadn't had a dead father who, instead of leaving his son in peace, came to see him every night demanding that he avenge his death. Me, I think the dead should stay in their place, and not entertain themselves by playing ghosts. The father would talk about how he was murdered by his wife, the boy's mother, and by his brother, because the two of them were also in love and wanted to get married. Basically, the dead man is jealous of everybody else and wants to keep them from being happy. What a family. The father, after stupidly letting himself be murdered, wants his son to kill all the guilty ones. Like it's the son's fault, all these stories. So then, Hamlet abandons Ophelia. He kills his mother and his uncle of course, and gets killed himself. That makes four deaths in place of one. They're really brilliant, all of them. It's truly idiotic. Anyway, I don't feel sorry for them. They deserved it.

Only, there's Ophelia. She never had anything to do with these sad family stories. When she finds herself abandoned, she feels such great sorrow that she can't take it. So she goes crazy. Simple as that. In any case, that's what people believe, because she roams around all day singing songs that are as sweet and sad as she is, and the others don't believe that anyone who's suffering that much could sing like that. In reality, that doesn't prove anything, of course. Finally, though, everyone believes she's crazy. One day, Ophelia walks along a river, softly singing all the while. She sees tender flowers in the water, a floral waterway. She leans over to gather them and falls into the water. And since she can't swim, she drowns. Then she floats down the river, all spread out with her long blond hair in the flowers. Poor Ophelia. Me, I think she wanted to drown herself amid flowers. She was fed up with feeling all that pain and singing so much. She couldn't take it anymore.

When the bell for recess sounded, we all remained silent. The professor went out, his eyes sunk in the depths of his round glasses. Then that giant, idiot string bean Lydia spoke. As for her, her ideal was to be just like Ophelia, to love and be loved so deeply, then to die in the water lost among water lilies in bloom.

I left without saying anything because it's true there was nothing to say. But I can't stand it that she goes on dreaming of such things. That's never going to happen to her. She's too ugly. And even if she died amid flowers the way she wants, nobody's going to mourn her like Ophelia, because Ophelia is so beautiful and sweet, with all that long blond hair. I can't stand any of it.

Remembering beastly Lydia's water lilies hurt so much that I sat down. Daisy woke up and raised her head. I said to her, "Sleep, Daisy. It's me."

She gave a great big yawn and went back to sleep. I like hearing Daisy yawn. She makes a frisky, cute little noise. You'd think she was laughing, and maybe she does laugh. I felt better. I lay down and I tried to sleep, too.

I was almost asleep when I heard the voice of the little girl saying, "It's not true, Maman! I'm dreaming! Tell me I'm dreaming, Maman!"

That gave me quite a start. I hadn't been thinking about the little girl anymore. With all my might, I tried to think of other things, or to fall asleep. But there was nothing to be done. The little girl came back, with that scent of gasoline and burning rubber.

All of a sudden I had a thought. What if, instead of stopping, I had just kept going on my old bicycle? Would the accident have happened? Instantly my heart started pounding. Sometimes my heart goes a little crazy. The car on the road might have stopped to let me pass, the car on the road would have passed me. That's all. I tried very hard to imagine it. I was cycling without stopping in that crazy rain, accompanied by the sharp little shriek of my bicycle. The car on the road let me pass. The car on the road went calmly on its way. It never happened. It really never happened.

But I'd stopped. It was raining so hard; it was so cold. Water was streaming from my face, from my legs, from my bicycle. I was riding down a frozen river. So when I noticed the car on the road, I stopped. I don't know why. Because of all the water that was drowning my face and eyes. I saw nothing. All there was, a long time after, was the uproar of the sky breaking into pieces. And after that, the silence of the end of the world.

When they brought the little girl out of the car I didn't notice anything. One side of her face was covered in blood and the other, clean, living, and so soft. She hadn't even lost consciousness. I thought, it's nothing. She looked calmly from her free eye. The rain fell hard on her face and the bloody water flowed, thick, into her hair, her neck, before disappearing into the grass of the slope. I thought: My coat will get dirty. I am unforgivable.

People came and there was a lot of noise. Someone tried

to clean the little girl's face with a can of water and a hand-kerchief. The mother watched, her teeth were chattering, and she was holding her face with her hands to try to stop her teeth from chattering. I looked at her because it's sad to be unable to stop your teeth from chattering, and because she really looked like a drowned person with that rain streaming down all over her.

All at once, her hands let go of her face. She opened her mouth, raised her face towards the sky and let out a bizarre, continuous "Ah!"—a sort of rasping gurgle. That's when I looked at the little girl.

She was missing one whole side of her face. The eye and the cheek. In their place was a big uneven hollow. It was funny, how half of her face had become a skeleton. The people went away and silence weighed everywhere. I wondered if the eye and the cheek had gotten stuck somewhere in the car, or fallen on the ground, maybe gotten dirty. I thought they better find them right away before they got too dirty, or too dead, or before someone stepped on them. I told myself that again and again. But I stayed there, watching that hollow of a face, with the blood filling it all over again, and the rain beating down hard on it, like into a puddle.

The little girl shuddered. She began to say, almost calmly, "Maman, it's not true. I'm dreaming. Tell me I'm dreaming, Maman!"

She repeated that sentence and nobody answered. Then she said it again, shouting, very loud, louder and louder, starting to be scared, to be very scared. She shouted and nobody answered. She shouted in the rain that refilled her eye socket and her cheek with bloody water.

I picked up my bicycle, which I'd put down on the slope, threw a leg over it and rode off. I pedaled very fast, without even sitting on the seat, in that crazy rain that drowned everything. For a long time I pedaled. Night fell. Finally I stopped. I couldn't go on. Immediately, I felt like throwing up. I threw up in the ditch as far as possible from the slope, in order not to get it dirty. I wiped my mouth and nose with a handful of wet grass. When I had recovered a little, I went on my way again. I had to stop two more times to vomit. It was lucky it was raining so hard.

I wanted to know. If I hadn't stopped, would all of that have happened? Would everything have happened?

I realized I was crying very hard for no reason.

I thought it was ridiculous to cry like that, for no reason. So, after a moment, I made myself stop. My face looked like it had rained. But it was winter, far from the summer storms that feel so good when you stick your head into the wind and rain. I like to recall memories of storms and wind. Only, I don't do it too often. I don't have many good memories, and if I go on recalling the same ones, they get used up, and they're no good anymore. After that, there's nothing left.

I asked myself what I was going to do, when the time came. My father by now must have forgotten his anger and I could go back into the house quietly, as if nothing had happened. Usually that's how it is. I had suffered for so many hours in the icy rain and my father had said to me: "Get out of here." I didn't know what to do anymore. I'm an indecisive person because most of the things I do don't matter, and what I decide changes nothing. But now I'd had enough. I would head back to the high school without setting foot inside my house. Too bad. At once, I felt tremendously relieved, as relieved and free as if my father hadn't chased me away.

I petted Daisy's soft head. Not every animal is as welcoming as she is. I owe my best memories to her, to her and the dog we had before her. Milan. My father hanged him because he was old. He wasn't sick or anything. Just old. Dogs can get very tired, sometimes, like people, but you can't hang people when they're no longer good for anything. You can do anything you like to animals, hang them when they get old and tired. Milan had understood that he was no longer wanted at the house. He hid, walked with his head low, hardly barked at all anymore. I searched for him everywhere to feed him, but he didn't want to come near the house. He still wanted to live. On Christmas night, I told the dog to come back with us, nobody would do anything to him because it was Christmas. And then, the next day, the dog was hanging from the big beam of the shed, rigid, his long purple tongue dangling. I was still little, but I understood. I began to scream and scream. In the end my father beat me to make me shut up. I don't think I was able to make myself stop. My mother shut me in the bedroom, and I stayed there all day. The next summer, when the drought came and the first stream had almost dried up, I found a skull in the mud. I buried it under bunches of wild hazel branches. One day, Daisy would be too old and weary, she would hide, and my father would hang her in the shed. Nothing could be done to stop it.

I was sad, in the face of all the sad things that had already happened, and all the others still to come. When I start thinking about that, I'm as relentless as death. There was also my mother's shopping bag. When I left, I would leave it in the shed. I couldn't take the stolen things back to the high school, that would have been stupid. My mother would find them and surely they would make her happy, in spite of everything. I took them for her. I don't tell her, but I take them for her. For nobody else in the world would I do that.

It's too hard to steal and I'm so afraid. You can't have any idea how afraid I am. If anyone found me out, I'd be expelled from the high school. There's no place for thieves at the high school. The headmistress told us that at the beginning of the year. And it's true that there are no thieves at the high school, despite what everyone thinks. The objects that disappear, and there are lots of them, are things that I myself take. It's fun. So many things go missing that everyone thinks that everyone else is either a thief or a future thief. And I know that nobody steals.

When I bring things home, Maman doesn't ask me where I got them. She takes them, puts them any old place, and then she forgets them. Later, she finds them, or one of the sisters finds them, and they put them to use. Often, this irritates me. It's so hard for me to steal, because of this foolish fear that's always with me. But I know very well that at our house that's the way it is, so I don't say anything. It must be because of these marshes. Because we live in the heart of a land choked with wild waters, where strange, mute flowers grow, and ghost birds live that we only know by the cries we hear on the murkiest nights, and then there are those crazy mists into which the trees and our hills vanish; and, because we live in the middle of these watery lands without ever meeting anyone, I believe we no longer have any idea what life is like elsewhere, or if people and towns even exist elsewhere. When I come home with these stolen things, Maman doesn't ask me anything because she doesn't think I could go anywhere apart from the high school, beyond the marshes. She's gotten so used to my bringing her something whenever I come back that I might have to come home empty-handed to make her notice for once. But it's hardly certain. Maybe she simply wouldn't notice.

I'll leave the shopping bag at the front door of the house. Maman will find it more quickly than if I leave it in the shed. I dug around in it and pulled out my green blouse. I gave it a sniff. It didn't smell good. Of course, it was filthy. Usually I wash it as soon as I get home, spreading it out on a chair near the fire so it dries quickly, and the next day, I iron it. This time, I'll have to take it back to high school dirty. It's the only one I have, and I hate it for being so green. Totally green. At the high school, you're supposed to wear blouses with pink and black checks. It's required. So me, with my blouse in such a blatant shade of green, I'm a blot that clashes amid all that pink. I would have liked very much to have a pink blouse. But my dead aunt didn't have any pink clothes, and how could she have foreseen the need? I made my school smock out of cloth from my dead aunt's prettiest summer dress, of green cloth with a little shine to it. The only thing I could make out of it was a kitchen apron. To improve it, I sewed an eyelet border on it, which gave me a lot of trouble. It might have looked impressive on a chef, my apron, but at the high school, no. At the high school, what counts is the color, and the green of my blouse, which is quite green, looks even greener when it's the only thing that's green. It produces a weird effect. I understand that it's unpleasant for everyone. Maybe people thought I was trying to stir up trouble by wearing such an attention-getting smock. At the beginning, when I saw everyone looking at it with revulsion, I was horrified myself. And then, soon after, I mostly felt bad for the thing. It isn't its fault. I almost began to hate it in a friendly way. And then, well, we've gone through a lot together, there's no denying that. At the start of every week, the school supervisor would say, "You will get detention on Sunday."

This was because of the rules and the pink blouses. The supervisor doesn't have her job for nothing. When she told me that, because of my green blouse, I'd get detention every Sunday, until I had a pink blouse like everyone else, I thought for a moment. Then I went to see her and I said, "If I get detention, I won't ever be able to go home to get a pink blouse."

This was so obvious that I didn't get detention. But of course I was lying. Even if I did go home, I wouldn't have a pink blouse. It was already more than enough that I had a green one. But the supervisor couldn't know that, and I didn't explain it to her. It would have taken too long. I would have had to tell her how I'd gotten it, and my other clothes, and that these were my dead aunt's clothes. On the one hand, I was happy to have them. On the other, it's an odd sensation, putting on a dead person's clothes. Moreover, Maria hadn't wanted them. At first, I couldn't get used to it. I always thought about my dead aunt. I liked her very much, my aunt. She was beautiful and sweet. Very beautiful and very sweet. My other aunts, the ones who look like a row of candles in mourning, hated her. That makes sense, they're unbearable to look at. Now my aunt is dead. When I wear her clothes, I think of the worms that eat dead people. Where do they begin? How much time does it take them? It seems to me that, if I'm going to be eaten, I'd like it to be done quickly. When you're dead, maybe you no longer feel like defending yourself from worms. Maybe it makes no difference to you, being eaten or not. I'd like to know.

Nobody knows, of course, that my smock belonged to my dead aunt, and all the same, everyone hates it just as much as if they sensed it. One day I was called green cretin. That was a terrible day. What consoles me, when I think about it, is that that was the very day that Fanny brought me the licorice. It was like a long ribbon of licorice rolled up on itself. We would unroll a little and eat it during class. We ate so much of it, Fanny and me, that our mouths were all black and bitter. We laughed when we looked at each other and saw that our teeth were all black too. Then we laughed again and got punished by the math professor, who's a stupid, pompous man that all the girls are in love with. He struts, he talks about things that have nothing to do with math, windmilling his arms and twiddling his long pointy fingers. How stupid he is. The day he called me a green cretin, he said other foolish things, too. I remember he said that, once when they were in revolt, students had spontaneously adopted the customs of their Gallic ancestors, using trash can lids as shields. He made a lot of gestures, imitating them. Then I raised my hand and asked how they managed to find the lids to the trash cans afterwards, I meant the lid that belonged to each trash can. The professor flushed, made a sweeping gesture with both arms and said, "You are a little green cretin."

Everyone laughed because of my smock. Me, I started to think of the frogs back home, in the green slime of the little ponds. The professor added, "If what is said here does not interest you, there's nothing preventing you from leaving, obviously."

So I got up and went out in silence. Fanny got up too, and went out with me. That's how we became friends. We went to hide at the bottom of the courtyard, in a shed full of old logs that nobody ever uses, which smells of wood shavings, dust, and spiderwebs. We kept sucking the rest of the licorice ribbons until I felt sick to my stomach. That's when I told the story about all my sisters dying one beautiful stormy night, when lightning struck our house.

Because of all the issues surrounding these dead person's clothes I wear, I have to steal to make myself a wardrobe. Afterwards, I'll burn all my old clothes. How happy I'll be when I've burned them all! Nobody can know. If, because of my dead aunt, I can't burn them up, I'll bury them far away, deep in the earth, or drown them in a hole in the marshes. I don't know yet. Before I've stolen everything I need, there'll be plenty of time to think about it. I can't take the other boarders' clothes, they'll be recognized right away. I have to go to Prisunic. Anyway, that's better. There are so many objects in bulk in each section that, if I take one, there's no real change. And then, because they haven't been sold yet, they don't really belong to anyone. You can't call that theft, I'd say. In any case, it's not like I'm stealing from another girl. That's important. I do steal from the other boarders, obviously, but only every other Saturday, right before I get on my bike and pedal really fast towards home. I take a little money from the day students on Thursday mornings, to buy things on Thursday afternoons. I never have any money. At home they don't give me any. They don't have any.

At the high school, money is pretty easy to steal. I only take coins, ones that the day students leave deep in the pockets of their jackets or their coats. All they'd have to do is pay a little attention. But they don't, and the proof is that, so far, not one of them has missed a single coin. No doubt they don't even know how much money they have. Their parents give them some every day, they can't count it all. For the boarders it's different. They only get money once a week and after that, they have to make it stretch six days. Better to leave their pockets alone.

On Thursdays, I ask to go to the bathroom, no big deal, and I go to the cloakroom and check out the clothes. I shake them a bit, if there are coins in the pockets, they clink, and all I have to do is take them. I've noticed that there are very dirty girls whose pockets are full of old breadcrumbs, or handkerchiefs hardened into a ball. That's disgusting.

I came up with this method of stealing because, at the beginning of the year, the headmistress told us over and over, I don't know how many times, that it's officially forbidden to leave money in the cloakroom. The girls are breaking the rules, and so much the worse for them if I take their money; if only they'd listened to the headmistress, there'd be nothing for them to complain about. That's pretty good, I think.

From Fanny, I don't steal. She's my friend, even if she's rich. I'm very happy she's rich. She's so beautiful that you can't imagine her poor, like us, for example. If she'd been born poor she'd be less beautiful, or not beautiful in the same way. At the high school I've noticed you can tell the rich girls from the poor girls by their faces. They don't have the same aura, or allure. This is absolutely true, and I can prove it because I've gone through the pockets of practically every girl in my class.

I put my smock down and stood up. Daisy didn't even wake up. She was deep in sleep, miles away, no doubt. I wondered what she was dreaming about. I often ask myself foolish questions. That's how I am. In class, the professors get angry. They think I'm doing it on purpose to annoy them. It's not true, of course. But they get very angry and that bothers me. Especially the French teacher, the day she spoke about racism. She loves talking about racism. She says it's a topical subject, a burning subject, words like that. And it's true. In class there are Vietnamese girls who are more intelligent than the other girls, and black girls who are less. This causes a lot of problems and sometimes we fight. That day, while everyone else was arguing, I was telling Fanny about Daisy's adventures and the dogs who come from far away to court her when she's in heat. Daisy is a beautiful dog, all tawny and slender, and she has great success with all the male dogs in the area, they fight for her. I was telling this to Fanny, and above all how Daisy always chose the ugliest dog, a malingering, dirty dog, really quite ugly. But that's what Daisy liked about him. You never know. We laughed, talking about these things, Fanny and me. I was calm and contented, and then, all of a sudden, I started thinking about red ants and black ants. I'd read a story about red ants in a magazine at the library. I asked Fanny if red ants mate with black ants. Fanny didn't know. I raised my hand to ask the professor. At that moment, in a voice thick with emotion, she was telling the story of the awe-inspiring black man Toussaint Louverture, who wrote to Napoleon, even though he was black. The professor broke off and asked me what I wanted, and I asked her if she knew whether red ants mated with black ants. I understood at once that I should not have spoken because a silence fell over the classroom that was so cataclysmic that I sat down in fright. And then the girls started laughing like savages. The professor rose to her full height, red in the face, and shouted in her shrill voice, "This is unheard of. Unheard of."

After that, she made me copy out a ridiculous sentence five hundred times. She said, "An imbecilic task for an imbecilic mind."

I was very angry that she said that to me. I never said

things like that to her, and because she's a professor, she can say anything she wants to us. I didn't respond. I thought she might think I'd been making a stupid joke. She didn't know the stories about Daisy and her canine admirers that had made me think of ants, and I really did want to know whether red ants and black ants could mix, and what kind of young they'd produce, and all that. But I said nothing, and copied out the five hundred lines, paying attention to my penmanship. The other girls were furious with me. Even though they were only given a hundred lines to copy—for having laughed in class. The profs hate it when anyone laughs or is happy in class.

I had difficulty standing up on my swollen legs. All the same I walked toward the house. It was freezing. The hardened earth cracked under my feet. That made me happy. I hate the mud so much. It was very cold out, with a sky full of stars that gave the house a creamy sheen.

I put the shopping bag by the front door. Poor Maman. She was sure to be so terribly sad that I'd left without seeing her. I began thinking about that, and all at once I started to cry, I who never cry, for the most part. I went back to Daisy's bed at a run and I cried hard, so hard, my head in my dirty smock so as not to wake Daisy and her puppy.

5

I woke with a start. Clanking noises everywhere. In a moment, I understood. My father was milking the cows, and the pails and the cream strainers were colliding. Knowing that my father was so near made my heart beat even harder. I have a completely crazy heart.

Daisy stretched, barked loudly, and was up in a bound. I felt a surge of tenderness for her and once again I felt like crying. That was stupid. Nonetheless, I was happy that at last the night was over.

I asked myself what I was going to do. I no longer wanted to leave as much as I had before. My mother must be making coffee in the kitchen. In a little while my father would join her and they'd drink their coffee in silence, and my father would add a little brandy to his because he said it gave him strength. Then my father would go back to the barn to see to the cows and the calves, muck out the barn floor, and all the rest. My mother would stay by the fire, waiting until it was time to go look after the poultry and the pig. That's how it goes every morning, since always.

So I thought I could take advantage of the time my dad was working in the barn to go see my mother. I love my mother, I have to say; and just then thinking about her made me feel so terribly sad, a sadness you could cut with a knife. I would have liked to see my mother for an instant only, and then leave immediately. All alone in the dog's bed, I was so very sad. And then I remembered it all. My mother would start to cry, to beg, to beg again, and I would stay, and maybe my father would throw me out again. I didn't want that. I didn't want that any more. Better not to see my mother.

I decided not to see anyone and to leave. When my father went back to the kitchen to drink his coffee, I'd leave Daisy and head off on my bicycle.

Daisy came back. I rested my hand on her muzzle. With her cold nose, she snuffled all over my hand then took it in her mouth and nibbled it, without hurting me or anything. She's extraordinary, Daisy is. She pretended she was eating me and having a feast. What an actress! In the meantime, the puppy nursed, making greedy noises.

Suddenly my father left the barn. I hadn't been thinking about him at all anymore. I was afraid. I was afraid he'd come here, that he'd find me in Daisy's bed. And if he felt like beating me with a stick, I wouldn't be able to defend myself, burrowed into this hole. My heart got crazier and crazier.

I remembered something I did when I was still little.

My father and my mother were shifting bales of hay in the barn. Mice were fleeing, running all over the place in a frenzy. I caught one. I took it to the meadow, by the bank of the stream. With a stick I dug a deep hole in the earth and carpeted it with grass so it would be soft. I put the mouse there. I wanted her to make her nest there. But the mouse didn't want to, she wanted to get away. I pushed her back into the hole with my stick. But she didn't want to stay. Suddenly she started making unhappy little squeaks. I don't know what happened. I got up, and with the tip of my stick, I crushed the mouse. In the end, nothing was left but a pink and gray sludge. I went to sit on the bank of the stream and threw up into the water. I stayed there a long time, sitting there surrounded by sturdy mint plants, staring at the dirty water.

Seeing my father, I thought about that again. My crazy heart went wild and I felt like throwing up.

My father went into the kitchen. I got up, took my green smock and ran behind the barn, towards my bicycle. I didn't even say goodbye to Daisy. I couldn't take it anymore.

My bicycle was waiting for me. I reclaimed it with incredible joy. If it had been a person I would have rushed into its arms, carried away by tenderness, even though I don't like to show my feelings, which is something my mother always reproaches me for. But my bicycle is better than a person.

Amid all the grayness gripping the earth, I could see how poor and worn out my bike was. It's so old and so rusted that I feel worse and worse every time I use it, it's as if I were forcing a really, really old animal to keep on going when it's about to die: to keep on going, keep on going. If I didn't really have to use it, I wouldn't, because the frame is flaking so badly, you'd think it was going to crumble to dust. It's ridiculous to say, but my bicycle is in such a broken-down condition that I think about it like a person, I can't help it. I worry about it just like I worry about my little sister Antonnella, who's so sweet and frail. When it rains, it's terrible for me because I know rain could kill it, rusty as it is. Some days I can't bear having so much to worry about. Other people are lucky. Fanny has never had to worry about a blind, frail sister and a bicycle devoured by rust. You can tell from her shining face. Fanny is bright as the sun in springtime. Me, I'm like a well in the marshes. It's terrible to be like me.

I took my bicycle and carried it up to where the path begins, behind the barn. It's a downward path, bordered with thick hedges full of old abandoned nests. No risk of my father seeing me.

The wheels of my bike were crusted with mud, and the mud had frozen during the night. I laid the bike down on the slope and sat down on the ground. My green smock bothered me. I rolled it into a tight ball and put it in my dead aunt's raincoat. At least the smock would be safe. Incredibly green and ugly as it was, I felt sorry for it, too. It's not the smock's fault. I lingered there a while, with the thick grayness of the world everywhere, and the mist from the marshes. It was very cold.

When I stood up, my feet and hands were numb with cold. I had nothing to wait for, not even the sun, which wasn't coming up. I hate how dark it is in these parts for months, day and night. Later on, when I'm grown up, I'll leave; I'll go to the land of wild sunshine, and there I'll be beautiful, too.

I found a stick in the hedge and started prying off the encrusted mud on the wheels of my bike. It came off in fat, rocky chunks. I'd promised myself that the next time I came home I'd take the back mudguard off of my bicycle because there was no way I could keep this up. Once the mud was off, I lifted up the front of the bike and then the back, spinning each wheel, making sure they turned smoothly. They screeched a little, but when I sat down it got better. When I'm sitting on my bike and we're moving, it squeaks. It squeaks, and that suits me, because it's got no bell to make our presence known when necessary. Also, it always reminds me of the story of the salamander.

This is a story from a long time ago, when I was still very little. One day my father went to hunt frogs in the big pond in the meadow. Whenever I remember this, and it's when I'm on my bike that I tend to, I can see that sunny spring that we'd had up till then, and all the vines and the marshes beyond them rustling with wild tulips, the fields and the ditches gone wild with flowers and all their mingled scents. And then, that Thursday, my father went to hunt frogs in the pond. He was fishing for frogs when, all of a sudden, a salamander appeared. He didn't want to take it off the hook because they say salamanders burn you if you touch them. He went back to the house with his sack of frogs in one hand and his fishing line in the other, held out at arm's length, with the little salamander dangling from it. He put the line on the pear tree in front of the farm. I didn't know. And then, just like that, I heard a cry, a kind of prolonged one-note squeak. A tiny little cry that seemed like it would never end. I looked around, and when I understood, I begged my mother to detach the salamander or at least to kill it very quickly. She didn't want to. She forbade me to touch it, it was a dirty beast, it'd burn me if I touched it. I sat under the pear tree near the squeaking salamander so it wouldn't be all alone. It squeaked continuously for a day and a night. It died all of a sudden in the morning.

I started walking along the path, pushing my bike, which was as yellow with mud as if it had been dipped in a slimy bath. That made me laugh—because of my grandmother. My grandmother, my mother's mother, had such bad rheumatism that she couldn't walk anymore. But Maman told me she went to take mud baths that totally cured her. What makes me laugh is the thought of someone holding my fat grandmother, stark naked, by the hands, dipping her in the muddy water, hauling her out, dipping her again, over and over for a long time, while she went on chanting her prayers. I would have liked to see that. I don't like my grandmother.

White patches of ice had filled the ruts in the path. I put my bike down again and entertained myself by breaking the ice with my foot. When I was little, I liked to do that a lot, to see what was underneath. Of course, there was never anything but emptiness. I didn't understand why. Most of all, I didn't understand why, when ice forms, it leaves a pocket of empty space between the ground and itself.

I took a piece of ice and rubbed my hands, cheeks, nose, and chin, which were very cold. That warmed me up a bit, but not much. When you're cold, you're cold. I walked to the stream to get a drink. I was thirsty, in spite of the cold. The stream was flowing quietly, the way it always does. I cupped my palm and drank a little water from the stream, like the time I was so thirsty on my way back from the village school, and stopped in the marshes to drink, among the tuffets of wild grasses, my heart racing a little because of my fear of leeches. I was sorry that the stream wasn't frozen over. In books, they talk about frozen lakes that you can slide and walk on as if you were on solid ground. Me, I'd be afraid of the ice breaking—that I would die from being drowned or frozen, trapped in the ice. I don't want that. Often, as I head to the high school on my old bike, I imagine how I will die. I thought about that in the past, too, but a lot less.

Sometimes on the road, when it's dark in winter, and in winter it's always dark, I make believe that the passing cars can't see me. My bicycle has no headlamp or bell to make us stand out. One day, at a bend in the road, a car will come that won't see me. It will hit me without even knowing it, throwing me into the air, and no matter how much I scream, nobody will hear. Everything will be like that. The car will come around the bend very fast, won't see us, my bicycle and me, and will hurl us up in the air, without even knowing it. We'll fall back down. There'll be a little bloody heap on the road. Nobody will ever know it's me, and I will have disappeared completely, once and for all, just like that, for nothing, like a bit of mud.

When I start thinking like this, everything becomes unbearable.

I was so full of sorrow all of a sudden that I wanted to go home, to go into the kitchen to the warmth by my mother and the scent of coffee. Maybe my father wouldn't say anything. I looked toward the house. Nobody was there. I waited to see if my mother would come out. Ordinarily, when it's very cold, my mother comes out with a pail of hot water for the chickens. But she didn't come out. All the shutters stayed closed. True, it was still early. Then I felt so sad, so sad, that I gave up the idea of going back to the house. Too bad.

I picked my bike back up and walked down the path, pushing it along the stream.

I crossed the wooden bridge over the stream. The sound of my steps and the squeaking of my bicycle mingled, and suddenly I had the impression that another person with another bicycle was crossing the old bridge the same time I was, and the four of us would meet there by accident. I liked this idea so much that I walked back across the bridge, then back again, several times in a row, and every time I ran into somebody. Eventually I stopped believing that. Since there was just me, it was stupid. Still, for a while, I was so happy.

I really like this stream. When I was small, in summer, there wasn't much water in it, and I would kill time walking up it. I wanted to know where and how it began. I never found out. It was too far away. But what I loved best was the sound of my voice echoing under the bridge. I'd pretend to be two people, I'd speak to the other person, who'd say the same thing back to me, and I would answer, and so on. I liked that a lot. Fanny laughed when I told her about it. I also liked to dance on the bridge, singing the song, "They Give a Ball on the Bridge of Nantes," because I believed it really was the Bridge of Nantes. That's still my name for our old bridge. I didn't name the other bridges, but I should have. It's important for every thing to have its own name. I should think about naming the other bridges. There are three, one for each path and the stream it crosses. It's good that there are all these bridges. At our place you'd think you were in a fortified castle surrounded by drawbridges. The bridges aren't drawbridges, but the planks are so worm-eaten that they'd fall to pieces if a stranger ventured on to them, he'd find himself in the water, drowned before he even knew it. Anyway, nobody comes to our place. You'd have to be out of your mind.

Sometimes, all the same, I felt sorry about that. Particularly that time when I threw the dead moles into the village well and the water started smelling so bad. I was still little. The village women shouted and threw stones, they shouted that they'd tell the police, who were going to come to our house to punish me. I waited for them by the bridge for many days, hidden in the hedge that borders the stream. They didn't come. It's a pity. I would have like to see it when they all fell in and drowned.

At last I came to the edge of the wood, close to the marshes. I really like this place. In the summer, the hedges grow dark with blackberries; in winter, the path is covered with crackling leaves and the debris of rusty branches. I really like this place.

I stopped. It was pointless to hurry, I had all day to cover the twenty miles on my bicycle. I put my bike down on the bare blackberry bushes, I wasn't worried about the thorns because the tires are solid. With normal tires, if they got a puncture, I'd be stuck in the woods, or, worse, on the road. I hate the road.

I couldn't stop thinking about my mother, and I realized it must be because I was so hungry. What was she making to eat, I kept wondering. Sometimes on Sundays she makes a special treat. When she thinks of it, or when I'm good. Then she says, "I made it for you, Galla, my Galla." Always the same words and then, just like that, I'm not hungry at all, and I want to kill the whole world so nobody will ever say things like that to me ever again.

My mother's special treat is boiled chicken. We don't get it a lot because the chicken has to be an old one, and they take their time. When they're finally old enough, when they're all drab and losing their feathers, you kill them and you cook them a really long time. It's nice. We spend the entire Sunday in the savory kitchen, knowing we'll get to eat our fill.

On Mondays at the high school, the girls talk about what they ate on Sunday. They're stupid. They eat exquisite things, so they say, with guests who arrive with cakes, wine, and dogs. Afterwards, they have stomachaches. Serves them right. Me, I don't say a thing. Besides, I don't like cake.

I went into the woods. I wanted to see if the rowan tree still had berries. That's not likely because birds get hungry too. My father says that foxes will eat berries, when they're hungry. Poor foxes. It must be unbearable to be a hungry fox, even worse than being a hungry girl. I gave up on the idea of going to see the rowan tree. I kept on walking through the woods, toward the top of the hill.

Walking along, I kept thinking what the girls say about the animals they have at home. One day I talked about this in a homework assignment. The first day. We were supposed to talk about an animal we like a lot. It was an idiotic subject. I love all animals. I said that people who neuter dogs or cats so they don't stray or smell bad are criminals. If they don't like animals the way they are, they should leave them alone. I got a bad grade. The professor explained to me that they neuter cats because cats are careless, and when they go out on the prowl they can get run over. But I said that if a tomcat wanted to risk his life for a female, that was his right. People have that right, and sometimes, when they're in love, they love each other so much that they die of it, like Tristan and Iseult, or like Inês de Castro. I read their stories in the high school library. The girls laughed. The professor said, "I see very well that you will never understand."

I said, "Yes."

Everyone laughed. I said to my classmate behind me, "Mummy-face."

It was true that with all her teeth and her gums flashing

in the air, Lydia looked like the mummies at the carnival. That shut her up. The professor heard me and gave me a line to copy out a hundred times: "I must not insult a classmate who hasn't done anything." I thought this was a slyly worded sentence, and it made me laugh. The professor thought I was laughing at her and doubled my punishment. I didn't say a word. Professors always think you're laughing or talking about them. There's nothing you can do about it.

I reached the top of the hill. On the other side of the hill and the marshes, the soil is beautiful, a miraculous soil, my father says. And it's true. It's beautiful black soil that faces the sun, without any mists, and everything grows in it. I've often gone there in summer to pick grapes, in winter to dig the wild leeks that grow among the vines without anyone needing to tend to them. In the bleached-out soil at our place, the only thing that grows is stones. Others harvest their crops, we gather our stones. We gather them one by one, painstakingly. We dig in the earth to flush out the ones that are hiding. We put them in piles at the edge of the fields, and the piles are enormous. You think you're all done. And then, as soon as my father starts working the soil, other stones appear. The earth secretes them. We gather them again with care, we hunt them as if we were panning for gold, we dig them up unstintingly. And they always come back. Everything dies in our blanched land. But the stones flourish. With all the stones we've gathered, you could build all the pyramids and bury yourself inside. At home, as soon as we open our eyes, we see the stones, we curse the stones, we bewail the stones. Always.

My father said we would buy good land. One day we

would buy good land. But I know we will never buy a thing. Those promised lands are not going to come.

It was those promised lands that kept laughter from our home. At the time of the harvest, a harvest that was always so meager, and that we always knew was going be meager, though we kept on hoping anyway, everything got so sad that all anybody could do was cry.

What I want to do is to study, to travel, to have money. One day I'll come back home with all my money. I'll give it to my father to buy land far away from these pale hills and wild waters. After that, I'll go away forever.

I ran back through the woods to my bicycle. It was waiting for me in the same spot. It's very loyal, my bicycle. I'm sorry that it ended up with a companion like me, who comes and goes like a spinning top and never knows what she wants. It's irritating. I know myself, I've lived with myself for fourteen years. If I had me for a friend, I wouldn't stick by me for long, that's for sure.

After thinking about my parents and their miserable life, I was so unhappy and felt so sorry for us all that I made up my mind to go back home, to at least take the time to kiss my mother and tell her how much I love her. I grabbed my bicycle and went back the way I'd come, fast, to keep from thinking. Luckily there was a hard freeze.

At the bridge, I stopped to look at the house. There was nobody outside, but the chimney was smoking. My mother was sure to come out into the yard to water the chickens. And if I stayed on the bridge, she was sure to see me, and because it was me she'd recognize me. Then she'd drop her bucket, and maybe it would spill, and she'd run to me with open arms: "Galla, my daughter, here you are, my Galla!" It's always the same, and usually that annoys me, but this time, I feel sure, it would have made me so happy.

I sat on the edge of the bridge, legs dangling. I amused myself by swinging my legs to the rhythm of a song I liked, "Cut the mistletoe, cut the holly." At this time of year I always sing that one. Christmas is coming.

I told myself that in the afternoon I'd go look for mistletoe with Rosine. Rosine is the sister who comes right after me. Every year at this time, I drag her off to look for mistletoe. At the beginning, Rosine grumbles a lot and says all the bad words she can think of, and she knows a lot. But soon enough she gets over it and is even happy. Then the two of us ramble all over the countryside, the woods, everywhere, until we find the mistletoe. We bring back armloads of it, all sticky with smashed berries, to bring good luck to our home so everything will go better. Nothing ever does, but who can say what might have happened without the mistletoe.

Along the way, Rosine and I interrupt our rambles to visit abandoned birds' nests. We always hope to find an egg that's been left behind, or a bird. There's never anything. Rosine says she likes exploring the nests more than gathering mistletoe. Then I have to explain that the nests don't bring good luck, and she doesn't get it, and it makes her laugh. She's still little.

The thought of gathering mistletoe with Rosine made me all happy. I looked over at our house. I was eager for my mother to come out so I could go in. Mentally, I called out loudly for my mother, so that at last she'd come out. The yard remained empty. Thick dark smoke poured from the chimney. They must be using wood that's too green. That smokes up the kitchen, and everyone gets red, burning eyes. The wood is always too green at our place. When I was little and we were burning green wood, I'd stay by the fireplace for ages. I'd watch the foamy sap coming out of the logs, making a shrill little whine like the cry of the little dead salamander. I thought it was tears and that the living wood was crying because it was dying. When at last it stopped crying, I ran away from all those tree cadavers lying in the fireplace.

My mother wasn't coming out and I decided to leave again. I had time, of course. But I'd had enough of stupidly waiting for her. Always waiting. Me, if I'd been my mother, and my daughter was waiting for me on the bridge, I'd have felt it. My daughter would have been in the house long ago. Even Daisy, who's only a dog, would have felt it. She's a very good mother, Daisy.

And that's when, all of a sudden, right when I was about to get up and go, I remembered my little dead sister. I have a dead sister, Cendrine. I hadn't thought about that forever.

It happened a long time ago. I was five and she was three. She was so little, my little sister, so slender and transparent that you could hardly see her. And if she walked you couldn't hear her. Or you'd hear a light rustling, like snow falling, and suddenly there she was, looking at you with her big eyes, dark and direct.

We loved each other so much, the two of us, that we were always together. When I was off at school with that great big pest Maria, she'd wander everywhere calling in her little bird's voice, "Lala! Lala!"

That's why she died. Really, that's why. I don't want to think about it, it's unbearably unfair.

It was in summer, a brutal August. Cendrine and I were watching the cows in the meadow over there by the stream. It isn't even a meadow, really, just a strip of land bordered on one side by the stream and wild mint, and on the other, that year, by a field of corn. The cows were so famished that the corn drove them crazy. Really crazy. They ran here and there and everywhere trying to get to that corn, and I ran everywhere too, with my stick, to try to keep them from eating it. It was a crazy time, and I understood very well how hungry they were.

My little slip of a Cendrine wanted to help me, and armed with a stick that was much bigger than she was, she ran everywhere, too. She was so slender and light that she looked like a fluttering wagtail. From time to time she called out "Lala" and I waved to her.

I have no idea how it happened. I think it's simply that the cows were too hungry. My father says hunger can drive people and animals mad. It must be that. I just don't know. It's unbearable.

Suddenly, a cow lunged, head lowered. My little sister flew across a great chunk of sky then fell back down into the cornfield. For a long time I looked at the empty sky. Then I was running after the cows again, they were already starting to eat the corn.

I waited for my sister to come back. She didn't come back. I called her. She didn't come back. Then I thought she must have hurt herself and gone back to the house, or that now she was afraid of the cows, that was also possible. That happened to me once, when the same cow hooked me with its horn and tossed me into the stream. I'd fallen near the bank, and I was able to hang on to some blackberry bushes. Otherwise I would have drowned. Or the water might have carried me far away, far away. I don't know. Back then I was really sorry the water hadn't carried me away. I didn't know. Then again, maybe I still really wanted to live. When you're little, you don't understand.

Since my little flower of a sister must have gone back home, I didn't worry. I continued chasing the cows. At night, when I brought them back and didn't see Cendrine inside the house, I started shouting and running towards the cornfield. Shouting. Shouting so loud that my mother followed me. We found my wagtail rolled up in a ball with her little legs stiff as the claws of dead birds in winter. Her big eyes, dark and direct, were still open. Perhaps she simply didn't want to live anymore, and she'd used this excuse to die. I don't know. With children you can never know.

I don't remember what happened afterwards very well. I only know that my father didn't beat me. Still, it definitely was because of me that my sister had died. I shouldn't have taken her with me. But we loved each other so much, both of us, that we always wanted to be together. Always.

I would have liked them to bury her on the bank of the stream, beneath the wild hazels, where the two of us used to sit. I'd tell her stories or play with her to cheer her up, because of her dark, direct eyes that were always so serious. We didn't believe in the stories or the games, but we pretended to laugh. We were good together.

My little sister, she was like a sad bird that loved me, and that I loved.

I would have really liked them to bury her by the stream, under the wild hazels. But Maman said no, we had to take her to the cemetery with all the other dead people, it had to be that way. I didn't want that, I said it would be awful, as little as she was, to find herself alone with all those dead strangers. But there was nothing to be done, we had to take her to the cemetery.

The day of the burial, they put her in her box. Afterwards, they put it on the cart to carry it to the village. On the coffin, Maman laid a very white sheet that we never used, her wedding sheet, Maman said, crying, which she had embroidered with horns of plenty. We also put flowers on the cart, water irises, because in the month of August there aren't very many flowers in the fields. Me, I sat on the cart next to my little sister. I started singing all the songs that we had sung together. I sang at the top of my lungs. She really liked to sing, with her little rippling voice. Maria sniggered. Nobody said anything to me. Anyway, the old cart, my black aunts, the family made a racket to scare off demons. As for me, I had the right to sing if I wanted to.

In the village, we were stopped by my teacher and the girls from school with fans of white flowers. We put them on my mother's wedding sheet and on the cart. There was no more room for me to sit. I left my little sister and I went to wait for her in the cemetery.

The hole dug for my sister was just beneath a cluster of cypresses, beside the wall. I was happy. Cendrine liked trees a lot, and it would certainly please her to have them near her, even in the cemetery. I climbed the wall and straddled it in the sun. It was very hot. To pass the time I picked hollyhocks and wild carnations from the wall. Carnations have an intoxicating peppery scent. I threw the flowers into my sister's grave. And then I sang all the songs again, and when I'd finished, I started over. I sang really loud, with all the sunshine and the crazy scent of the carnations.

At last the others arrived. Men were carrying my sister on their shoulders. It made me laugh. She was so tiny, so transparent, my little sister, that I could have carried her all alone.

When the schoolmistress saw me straddling the wall, she came up to me. I hate her. She said, "Get down from there at once."

I didn't budge. I kept on singing for my sister. We weren't in school. Then she said, "You have a heart harder than stone."

I said nothing. Me, I know how cruel *she* is, my teacher. I kept on singing a little longer. Then I jumped down from the wall on the other side and walked home, taking my time and singing at the top of my lungs.

I stopped by the bank of the stream, in the sunshine. I peed in the water, like my little sister. When she peed in the water, she would say, "Look, Lala, I'm making a little stream."

She was light and gentle as a little bird, my little sister. We loved each other so much that we always wanted to be together.

Now she's dead.

I picked up my bicycle and rode back and forth on the bridge, trying to believe that I was bicycling to meet my sister. But I couldn't.

So I walked along the path, into the woods.

6

I STOPPED by the edge of the woods. I laid my bike down in the thorny blackberry bushes. I paused for a moment to think about what I was going to do and then I went into the woods. I wanted to find a little juniper tree. I decided that this year we would have a Christmas tree in the house like all the other houses have. We've never had a Christmas tree. There was no point because Santa Claus never came to our house. When I was little I didn't understand. I wondered what terrible things we could have done to justify Santa Claus neglecting us so completely.

He did come one year, though. The year when my aunt, the one who died this summer, came to spend Christmas with my grandmother. I hate my grandmother. That year, Santa Claus brought me a book. *The Little Match Girl*. It's a beautiful story. In the end, the little girl dies but she's happy to die. I read it so many times that I still know it by heart. My sister Maria, who's a great big jealous pest, took it from me and hid it in a hedge. When I found it, much later, it was ruined, you couldn't read anything anymore. It was the only present I'd gotten in my entire horrible life. I didn't say anything when I found it again, totally ruined. Maria would have been too happy. And besides, I never cry.

Afterwards, on winter nights, I'd tell the story of the little match girl to my sisters. They got to know it by heart, too, and fell into the habit of pretending to be the little match girl. When I found out about that, I told them to stop it and slapped them. They started up again all the same, and I ended up leaving them alone. Little kids like that, they don't understand. I often forget that they're little. That's the way I am.

This year, they'll be happy that we have a tree and presents. Fanny is helping me. She's a marvelous girl, Fanny. She always understands everything, even when she doesn't understand. And then, how beautiful she is, with all that golden hair that ripples over her shoulders. If I had been loved, maybe I would have been beautiful, too.

Fanny and I are getting Christmas ready for my family. We're knitting gloves, red for my mother, blue for my father. I'll give that great big pest Maria the scarf Fanny brought me one day, a pretty, multicolored scarf with long fringe. For the little ones, it'll be a rag doll each. Fanny, who doesn't know that I have sisters, she still believes they're dead, thinks it's to decorate my bedroom. It makes me laugh to think about it. Because at home, we all sleep crammed into two beds, head to toe, and the walls of the bedroom are crumbling from the damp. My father says they're tainted by the quarry sand they're made with. Me, I don't know. I like the sand a lot. It's a nice pale gold, very soft to the touch. What's for sure is that in that bedroom my dolls will soon be ruined.

Fanny brought rags and scraps of cloth for the dolls. During recess and on Thursdays, we make the dolls. The other girls in class thought it was a good idea, and now they're all making dolls. They're stupid.

Shuffling through the dead leaves, I found some old chestnuts. I shelled them and ate them. I like chestnuts a lot, raw or cooked. Maman cooks them at Halloween every year. In the past, when the grandmother that I hate with all my heart lent us her pierced pan with the very long handle, we roasted them on the fire. Now, my grandmother won't lend us her pan anymore, I don't know why. She's so mean. We eat the chestnuts boiled. That's good, too. Even raw they're good. Me, I'm always so hungry that I would eat anything. That's how I am.

I found a cluster of little junipers, all covered in frost. I'll make a pretty little Christmas tree out of them. At Prisunic, I'll take some candles, that's easy this time of year, there's always a lot of people around. Everyone at home will be surprised and happy, even my father.

I went back to my bicycle. It was wrong to abandon it like that, all alone in the bushes. One day someone's going to steal it from me. There are always madmen. It's inevitable, as my French professor says, who always uses the same words, so reliably that I entertain myself by counting how many times she says them in an hour. She says "do you understand" and "isn't that right" close to sixty times; "inevitable" ten times; and when she's angry she says: "it's unheard of." I think I'd be happier if she swore. Obviously, because she's a French professor, she can't. But I think it would be less sad. Too bad.

For a while I walked down the path, pushing my bicycle and listening to the crackling of dead leaves. The earth was hard with frost, even the trails in the marsh. I was afraid of running into the old Spaniard with the goat, so I ran through the clumps of frozen bulrushes and water irises. My bike bucked and squealed nonstop. For once, I would have liked it to shut up. Poor bicycle. It wasn't easy running, because of the weeds and the holes that I was scared would make me trip and fall. But I didn't fall. And in any case, I don't think anyone was in the marshes, not even the sullen birds.

By the time I finally reached the road, my heart was beating like crazy. Nobody was going by. It made me terribly sad, that lonely road. I thought that a road without cars or bicycles wasn't a road anymore. It was lucky for the road that we were there, my bicycle and me, otherwise, what use would it have been? It used to be a gravel road, without tar. I was still small.

Sometimes, I enjoyed coming up here just to see who was going by. If it was cars, I threw sticks at them. I didn't throw anything at tractors or bicycles. Somebody could have seen me before I had time to run away. I went back home as proud as if I'd traveled all the way to the source of the Amazon. It seems nobody's ever done that. When I was little, I thought everything beyond the marshes that protected our house was enemy territory, since everybody from there always chased me away as soon as they saw me. They know I'm the one who makes things disappear from their places. They never caught me, so I don't understand how they found out. But I know they know, because as soon as they see me they throw rocks at me.

Everything started after the terrible story of the cows and the cornfield, that year when they were so hungry and we were, too. I understood how hungry they were, and that you couldn't reason with them or slap them or kick them like my father does to me when he wants to teach me a lesson.

Those cows and me, since we were always together—me watching them, them trying to get away—we'd become friends in a way. We'd gone through some very hard times together, really hard. Through them I understood that everything my father said about honesty, and about how you must never owe anything to anybody and all the rest, was nothing but lies. Lies and nothing else. Once I understood that, I set about making things a little less unjust, without telling anyone about it. The cows had nothing to graze on but stones and earth, and there was no reasoning with them, so I went out to see how things worked in other places, over on the other side of the hedges and the marshes. I'd grab some cornstalks, or ears of corn, or beets—basically, whatever the cows like. In the meadow, together, we ate the beets and the fresh, creamy ears of corn.

I did my runs at noon. At our place, meals went by fast. While the neighbors were eating, I'd hunt food for my cows. It made sense. That's why none of my sisters got eaten. Because, more often than not, I had to take care of the littlest child when I was looking after the cows. I'd take her with me, her and the straw-filled box she slept in, and set it right in the middle of the meadow so I could see her from wherever I was. From time to time, a cow would approach and inspect the box. The little one would wail. The cow wasn't all that hungry. She was happy to eat some of the straw sticking out around my sister.

I've always thought that if I'd tended pigs instead of cows, everything would have been different. Sometimes pigs eat their own young, baby chicks, everything they can get. They're always hungry. At our place there's a pig or two, but penned up. Whenever you go by their sty, they raise their eyelids and stare. My mother says they think they're at the theater. When she's the one passing, they squeal so she'll fuss over them. They know she likes them a lot. She's always gotten along well with all her pigs, except for once, when she had a couple of serious run-ins with one of them. She'd gone to change its straw, and afterwards, she'd rubbed its stomach as usual, and up to then, all the pigs loved having their stomachs rubbed. Nobody could figure out why the pig did what it did. It turned around and bit my mother on the thigh, really hard. If she'd been passive, it might have eaten her up, along with the other pigs, there's no telling. Me, I think this pig didn't like being touched, and that day, it had had enough. Animals, like people, have their own personalities.

My mother was so devastated by the pig's bad behavior that when it came time to kill it that year, on January 21, she didn't even cry, and she even came to see it get its throat cut. My mother is terrible. Sometimes she makes me laugh. In my opinion, she was sort of in the right. She always treated her pigs perfectly. For example, if she has a visit from my grandmother or my aunts, I hate them all, she never fails to take them to see the pigs. Afterwards, the visitor comments, compares her pig to my mother's, the size of their rumps. In the end, my aunts always decide that their pigs are prettier than my mother's and they're loud about making that known. When they're gone, my mother is angry, sometimes sad. She can tell that the aunts don't love us.

Me, what I would have liked, every time, would be for my mother to throw my grandmother and all the aunts into the sty with the pigs and let the pigs devour them. That's what I would have liked.

I straddled my bike and started pedaling vigorously to buck myself up and get the blood moving in my frozen legs. I tried to sing a little, I knew it wouldn't work, my heart felt like a sack of gravel. I couldn't sing. When I'm in a mood when I really need to sing, I can never find my voice. Things can be like that, you don't have something at the moment you need it. My voice was a stranger's, and I stopped trying to sing.

Plus, there was black ice on the road. I knew that, obviously. But I'm the kind of person who never picks up on danger until I've jumped into it with both feet. Like, if I'd been a soldier during the war, I wouldn't have figured out that a war was really on until the enemy blew up my head like a bloody firework. That's me.

So in this case, it was only when my bicycle slid and the two of us found ourselves sprawled on the frozen grass of the slope, me underneath, the bike on top, that I got it: black ice. Luckily, my bike didn't break anything. Poor bicycle. I promised I'd be careful. My bike is like certain little old people: so frail that the tiniest thing can break it.

I stayed there for a while, sitting on the bank beside my bicycle. We needed a rest and I was in no hurry.

Eventually I decided to set out again. Maybe it was later than I imagined. Without a watch, under this gray sky on this gray land, how can you know.

Once again I mounted my bike, taking care not to jostle it. I pedaled, and noticed that the right pedal had got a little twisted in the fall, and that my knee hurt. To avoid falling again, I decided to go slowly. If the patch of black ice was small, I'd go around it, if it was big, I'd stop, and get around it by walking on the bank. That way I'd be sure at least not to break my bicycle, which is so precious to me.

This reminded me of the most recent composition I'd handed in at school. The subject was: "If you could take only one object with you to the desert, what would it be? Justify your choice." It was a completely cretinous subject, as usual.

As for me, if anyone were to demand that I go to the desert with only one object, I would ask to take nothing at all. But the professor absolutely insisted we had to take at least one thing. She's a maniac. Of course, she expected everyone to say they wanted to take one of the books she talks about, or a record. The girls in class said that, to please her and to get good grades. They all wanted to take *The Little Prince* or *Le Grand Meaulnes* or *The Old Man and the Sea* with them. Books like that. I think that's idiotic. When I love a book I've read, I remember it. There's no need to take it to the desert, I can just tell the story to myself if I want. I can even make up stories without a book. It's the same with records. When I sing it's always like someone else is singing. My voice is a stranger's voice. And when I see myself, I see a stranger, too.

I wrote this in my composition, though I knew what the professor wanted. Professors always want you to talk to them about the things *they* like.

Next, I thought about what I really could take, since I had to choose something. I had a lot of ideas. I thought of a big hat, because of the devouring sun, and then, I told myself that it would be good to die in the sun. Then I thought of a sheet to cover myself at night. I can't sleep uncovered, especially not with my head uncovered. But a sheet is cumbersome, and also, in the desert, I would quickly die of thirst. Unless a caravan passes and picks me up on one of the paths where the camel merchants travel, at the edge of the desert. But it's better not to count on that. Finally, the only good idea that came to me was my toothbrush. A toothbrush is useful, it's not cumbersome. I can easily picture myself walking in the dunes of the desert, my toothbrush in my hand. In moments of repose, I would put it down beside me, it wouldn't bother me. But on reflection, I rejected that idea, for very simple reasons.

First, in the desert, there's no water. I wouldn't be able to brush my teeth. Not that this would keep me from taking my toothbrush. But the more serious thing, the thing that made me decide to reject the idea, was that I'd risk losing it whenever there was a sandstorm. To find a lost toothbrush, even a red one, under a sand dune, can't be easy. The science professor explained to us that dunes shift during sandstorms. How could I know, then, which dune might have carried off my brush? And I know myself. I would never just go on my way, leaving behind an object I was responsible for, which had followed me faithfully. I'd be forced to stay behind for ages, turning over the sand, trying to find my brush. It would be a horrible ordeal. If I didn't find it, I'd stay at the bottom of the dune indefinitely. The next sandstorm would bury me, too. Maybe it would uncover my brush, and then it would be my brush's turn to wait for me. Things like that are awful.

This assignment really annoyed me. So, because I'd had enough of these stories our professor tells, I said that if I had to go to the desert with one sole object, it would be my bicycle. That's the way it was. I gave no reason. It was that or nothing. Furthermore, I hate this professor.

I pedaled very hard, determined to keep myself from thinking. I've noticed that as soon as I start thinking, I get upset. I was exasperated in the bitter cold, alone with my fragile bicycle, like in the desert, with all the houses locked up around their fireplaces. I wanted the world to break into pieces like the bitter pomegranates I stole from my aunt's gardens, which burst into a thousand red sparks when I hurled them with all my strength against the wall of my aunt's house because she didn't want me to steal her pomegranates. I longed violently for the world to explode in bloody fireworks. It didn't happen. Nothing you wish for ever happens. I know that all too well. It doesn't matter. If the whole red smashed-up earth were to explode in the pale sky, it would not be enough to console me. I would need to explode, too; to splatter the whole world like tears of rain. Nothing.

Then I pedaled. I pedaled and pedaled while listening to the little salamander squeak of my bicycle.

I went on like that, sometimes pedaling, sometimes getting off to gently guide my bicycle, and I thought, I'm holding its hand. I would have liked to be able to sing to cheer us up, but I couldn't. I was too tired. And filled with a sorrow that had no voice.

I thought of Fanny—I'll see her tomorrow. I repeated to myself: She's a marvelous girl, Fanny. I told myself: Everyone loves her. And it's true everyone loves her. I'm sure of it. Her hair and her green eyes are full of sunshine, you can't *not* love her. You'd say she was born for it. Me, I would have liked to be like her. But I will never be like her. I am her exact opposite. I don't even understand how she can like me. Me, if I were as marvelous as her, I wouldn't like me, I would hate me for being so dark, with that black hair, those dark eyes, and that kitchen apron that's so relentlessly green. Whenever I think about myself I hate myself even more than the others do. Much more.

When I first came to the high school, everyone made so much fun of me, even the professors, that I was like a ball furiously ricocheting off the walls. Then, Fanny came along, and Fanny, everyone likes her. Me, they don't like very much, but they don't make fun of me too badly anymore. Once

Fanny took me under her wing, they didn't dare. That's sad too.

There's one thing I'd like to do, when I think about myself. Something unbearable, which I wouldn't do to anyone else, not even to a toothbrush.

It came to me one day when I was in town, walking to Prisunic. On the corner of the road that leads to Prisunic there's a store with a big mirror that takes up an entire section of storefront. You can see yourself in it as you pass by in the street—as if from a distance, through a haze, because the mirror is so old. Everyone looks at themselves as they go by. Girls and boys often pause to fix their hair. Somehow, although I know the mirror is there, I never remember it. I don't know why.

One Thursday I glanced at the mirror, saw a girl approaching, and felt something like fear. Not exactly fear, more like a pain in my heart that hit me like a punch in the chest. I looked around. Nobody there but me. Again I looked in the mirror. The girl, motionless, looked back. Then I understood. It was me. Obviously. Who else could it be? Except I didn't recognize myself. All at once, for no reason, I felt totally bereft.

I gave up on going to Prisunic and got back on the road to the high school. While I was crossing the bridge across the river at the edge of town, the longing came over me. I violently longed to hurl that black-and-green girl into the river, that girl who stared back at me from the mirror and gave me such pain in my heart. I didn't want to die, no. Just to get rid of myself, not to kill; to rid myself of that girl from the mirror, so I'd never see her again.

I ran back towards the high school. I told myself it would

be enough to ditch the girl in the mirror, not to drown her, to strand her somewhere. To pretend to forget about her, the way you forget about a dog or cat you don't want anymore, that you abandon somewhere. And afterwards to go far away so she could never find me again. Sometimes, when you abandon a dog, it stubbornly comes back to the master who doesn't want it anymore, and then you have to kill it one morning at dawn. If I went to the desert, I would leave the girl by the dune where the toothbrush was buried, to wait forever and ever.

And then I would go far away. Alone at last.

Ever since I started trying to lose myself, this is how it goes. I feel sorry for myself, like I feel sorry for my green smock or my bicycle or the toothbrush I wanted to lose. I think about myself and tell myself that nobody wants me, not even me. Then I feel sorry for myself because nobody wants me, not even me.

I started pedaling furiously, without thinking of the patches of black ice, trying not to think at all. I couldn't take it anymore. Really, the thinking had to stop. I rode like that for a while, very fast. Then I calmed down. I had to stop, I came to a steep slope and I couldn't make it up on my bike. I had covered nine miles. I sat down on the slope. In my dead aunt's green raincoat there was no risk anybody would recognize me. Besides, nobody was driving past. I don't like to encounter people on the road. But here, in all this grayness, without anybody anywhere, it suddenly seemed to me that I was traveling through a cemetery without tombs. The thought left me feeling even more oppressed.

I advanced up the slope on foot, pushing my bicycle. From

the top of the slope I looked at my Aunt Emilia's house, which is set back a little from the road, in a hollow. I made sure she wasn't outside, then took a running start, hopped on my bicycle the way men do and burned past at top speed for fear she might come out. She didn't come out. If I was the only person in the whole wide world, and the only other living being was my Aunt Emilia, I would flee to the exact opposite end of the earth so there'd be no risk of ever running into her. Or kill her, to make doubly sure. Because my Aunt Emilia is the worst hyena in existence since the world was made. The worst. I know everything she's done because Aunt Gina, another kind of hyena, told Maman. Apparently, Aunt Emilia is making her husband sick with heartache over a lover. My uncle drinks to console himself, but my aunt doesn't want him to drink anymore. So much so that my uncle is heartbroken, either from drinking too much, or from not drinking. My mother says he's killing himself. Me, I don't know. I don't like my uncle much. He always says to me: "Hey, squirt, still got those nasty eyes of yours?" I hate that, and he's said it to me every time he's seen me since I was born. I can't get used to it. When something appalls me I can't get used to it. If, when I'm fifty, with loads of children and all, my uncle is still alive, he will not fail to say, "Hey, squirt, still got those nasty eyes of yours?" in front of absolutely anyone. It's really awful.

I know all the details of Aunt Emilia's affairs. Aunt Gina never stops talking about them and if she does stop she starts again because there's always something she forgot, so it goes on like that endlessly. My mother listens, her mouth open and moist, exclaiming as if it were something out of one of her romance novels. I hate Aunt Gina just as much as Aunt Emilia.

Soon Aunt Emilia's house was far behind me. Once again, I remembered the black ice. Then I fell. It's always like that. Things happen when you're afraid. It's as if you were calling for them. Luckily, nothing happened to my bike. As for me, I banged my knee again, which started to hurt a lot. Poor bicycle.

It kept going, though, with its relentless little salamander squeak. Me, the more I watched the road because of the black ice, the more stories I told myself.

After a certain point, there was no more black ice. I entered the valley and it wasn't as cold there.

7

I LIKE entering the valley because of the river and the trees along its banks. Also because of the rowboats and the sailboats.

People I don't know get to have all of that: the lowlands, the river, the boats. For us, it's earth sown with stones, marshes of crazy grasses, and three streams. If we'd lived in the river valley we'd be rich. That's what my father says. When I look up and down the river, at the houses with peaceful windows, I tell myself: If I'd been born in one of those houses, that would have been enough. But how can you know? How can you know what it would have been like if you'd been born someplace else? I've never seen the sea. I would have liked so much to be born by the sea and the sun. I was born in a remote place, deep in the country, under eternal fogs. I would have liked so much to be born in sea and sunshine.

Night began to fall. Really, day had never broken. Everything was so sad and weary, this deserted world, everything. The day hadn't had the guts to get up. Me, I would have liked to live in one of these houses locked around a fireplace, and not get up.

I started dreaming of sunshine so hard that it made my

arms and legs tremble. There are days when I dream like a fool about impossible things that make me fall to pieces. Here, on this stupid road, alone with my old bicycle and its dying-salamander squeal, the night weighing down all around me, unable to see anything anymore for lack of a headlamp on my bike, I started dreaming of sun-drenched lands, of sun on golden beaches, blue shadows, delirious perfumes. That's what I lived in hope of. A tune that our professor plays on the violin, "Harlequin's Millions," kept running through my head. Sometimes I'm crazy.

To chase away these thoughts and that flowery music, I pedaled even faster. I had to hurry if I wanted to get to the high school in time for dinner.

I thought about the girls at the high school who don't make fun of me as much as they used to, now that I'm friends with Fanny, and because I get good grades. I was almost happy that I'd be seeing them again soon. I remembered a story I read when I was really little. It was a long time ago.

It's the story of a little boy, Harlequin. I don't know any-more who his parents were, what they did or anything like that, but I know they were poor. Really poor. And then, one day, there was a fair. All the little boy's classmates were going to the fair, they had beautiful new clothes and everything they needed. The little boy, he wasn't going to the fair. His clothes were too awful, he wore nothing but rags. So, the schoolmistress asked all the children in his class to bring in scraps of cloth, it didn't matter what kind. Out of all those scraps, she created a suit for Harlequin. It was a suit made up of lots of little scraps of cloth, none of them matching. And everyone was happy. Everyone loved him.

I read that story when I was very little. I remember I'd

started dreaming that one day, a day like any other, I'd come to school and everyone would love me, they would have made me a beautiful suit of clothes of every color, like Harlequin's. It would be a day like any other, with the cold, the mud in the ruts of the paths, the wet feet. Then I would get to school and the suit would be there. Then everything would change. The days, even the marshes, would never be the same again. That's what I dreamed of. I was still a very little girl.

Later I laughed at my dreams. The teacher hated me. I had her as a teacher for a long time because there were only two teachers at my school. She hated me from the start. I don't know why. I hadn't done anything to her, or to anybody, I was so little. Maybe she resented me for being there. When you hate people, you resent them for being there, even if it's not at all their fault. I think that's how it was for my teacher. Also, she punished me. She wouldn't let me warm myself when I was so cold that I couldn't write. She would say: "Look how dirty she is. Don't get near her. Look how dark she is." This while I was right there. Later, when I drowned myself in the stream and she heard about it, she said: "Leave her alone. She's crazy." Was I crazy? I don't know. I was so little.

Now that I've left that school, this is what I recall. She didn't look mean. She was always dressed in black and her round, pink cheeks glowed. Even when she was at her cruelest, she had an air about her that was almost sweet. So I don't know anymore. Maybe she believed what she said. I just don't know. All I know is that she punished me, and she was happy.

Today, if someone gave me a Harlequin suit I don't know what I'd do with it. I believe I'd take the package and my bicycle. We'd ride a while, my bicycle and me. Then we'd go to the riverbank or home to the marshes. I'd drop the package with the suit in it into the water. I would drown Harlequin's suit. That's for sure. I would drown it.

On the road, it was getting darker and darker. I had to guide myself by the sounds my bike made, soft on the grass, hard on the road. Finally, I drove onto the shoulder. That was sensible. Otherwise, a car might run me over without seeing me, and afterwards, who would know it was me? It's really unbearable to have a bicycle without a headlamp at night. And nobody anywhere to call for help. Luckily, there wasn't a lot more road to cover.

For a moment, I dreamed of my mother. I would have liked to call her. It's been a long time since she responded when anyone called her. Too many sorrows. Maman doesn't even show interest in the little ones. At home, they get up when they can, they grow as they can. Maman doesn't get involved. We dress in whatever we can find, the little ones in the clothes of the bigger ones, the big ones in those of the little ones, me in the clothes of my dead aunt, so we always look like we're in costume, or like we're Bohemians, because practically nothing has ever been ironed. It looks strange if you're not used to it. When it comes to food, it's the same thing. We get by as well as we can. The little ones finish the big ones' bowls of bread in milk or gnaw any crusts that are left on the table. When there's nothing, they resign themselves to waiting. It would be useless to shout and ask for more. Maman doesn't move. She's grown so accustomed to the cries that she doesn't hear them.

The only sister who gets taken care of even a little bit is Antonnella, the tiny one. She can't see. If they didn't give her food to eat, she would perish. She's so delicate, so pretty with those soft little curls around her head, that everyone at home loves her.

Me, I taught her how to navigate on her own, to walk outside of the house without bumping into things or falling into the pond. At first she walked slowly with her little stick in front of her, and when she met an obstacle she would stop and say "the millstone," or "the wheelbarrow," or "the mower," like I'd taught her. Now, she knows how to avoid all the obstacles without her little stick, and when you see her run, light as a butterfly, you can't believe she's blind. Her happy, luminous eyes are livelier than eyes that see. They're like innocent periwinkles, Antonnella's eyes.

This summer I taught her about the marshes. It's going to be a long time before she can navigate them on her own. First of all I had to teach her how to identify and locate the faintest sounds, because of the old Spaniard and the goat who hide among the grasses and the reeds. I taught her how the sound of the wet earth beneath your feet tells you when you're on the edge of a water hole, or a slimy spot, or a reed-filled area where somebody might be hiding. I taught her to identify the sounds of the flights of birds, of water rats. And above all, I taught her how to crouch, motionless, and listen to the water bubbling in the sodden earth to find out if someone's walking in the marsh, like the old Spaniard with the goat, and whether he's near or far. Every day of summer vacation I went into the marshes with Antonnella to teach her. She still has a lot to learn. She's so little. Next summer I will continue the lessons, and then she'll figure it out.

I don't ever want the Spaniard to lie in wait for her among the wild grasses. Blind and delicate as she is, she wouldn't know how to defend herself. But I'll teach her. At home, none of the others knows the marshes, they don't know how to walk that secret landscape without getting bogged down, nobody dares enter. Sometimes, when she's angry or very sad, Maman says she's going to go drown herself in the marshes, and that nobody will ever find her again. She's never even been there. If she did go, she'd be sure to sink into the slime and drown. She'd have no idea how to save herself. Or maybe the Spaniard would catch her, and Maman, who's always so distracted, wouldn't know how to defend herself.

Thinking of this, I was suddenly filled with horror. I said to myself, yes, I will teach Antonnella to defend herself in the marshes. The old Spaniard wanders there all day long. He's there even when you don't see him. He's always there, alone or with his goat, and he's waiting, nobody knows for what. If he surprised my mother or Antonnella, they wouldn't understand, and they would die, and I would die, too. Already, Antonnella, who is so pretty and so proud of what she has learned, says with a laugh: "Tomorrow I'll go into the marshes by myself, Lala! I'm big."

No, no, I say. But sometimes I find her far down the misty path, and then I scold her and take her back home. She doesn't know the danger, she's so little and all. So I'm often afraid.

I started pedaling very hard to forget all that. I pedaled.

And then, there, all at once and for no reason, I began to feel truly afraid. I know myself. When fear like this takes me over, I'm scared of everything. Of the road. Of dark ditches and what might come out of them. Of treacherous waters that might catch and trap me in algae. When I'm afraid, I'm really and truly afraid. I'm overwhelmed by the irresistible desire to scream. But I don't scream. There's no one to hear me, and if anyone did hear me, nobody would put themselves out for me. That's to be expected. But inside, I'm screaming, shouting to myself: "Save me!"

I try to think of something I could do to save myself. This is hard, because, as my father always says, I go about everything the wrong way. What appears most important to me at a given time is never actually the right thing. For instance, if there were a fire in the house, and the most urgent thing was to get out of there, I might decide it was more important to finish a row of knitting, or close the curtains, or brush my teeth. Things like that, basically. Meanwhile, there's a fire.

That's why, when I found myself all alone in the pitch dark with all that fear washing over me, what came to my mind was Nicole. She's a girl from my class. Fanny told me all about her. Fanny knew the stories of all the girls, especially Nicole, they've known each other forever. She told me that Nicole's father left her mother one day for another woman. Ever since, Nicole's mother has repeatedly tried to kill herself, without success. That must be terrible. Nicole is always afraid that she'll come home from the high school one night to find her mother dying. At the high school, the girls are afraid that Nicole will imitate her mother. They seem so convinced of this that maybe she really will do it. It's as if Nicole were dead already. I think that's unbearable. If I were Nicole, I'd go ahead and kill myself to cut the suspense.

When Nicole wanted to give a presentation on Tristan and Iseult, the girls were worried. They thought that Nicole wanted to die like Tristan and Iseult, and this was her way of telling us. They are cretins.

And then, everything turned out fine. Nicole said Tristan

and Iseult were lucky because the most beautiful thing in the world was to die for love, and without that kind of sacrifice, love itself would die. The girls agreed. They all wanted to die for love. I thought that if that was the case, soon they'd all be dead. Me too, but not for love. I'll never love anyone because nobody will ever love me. So much the better.

Our professor, seeing that everyone wanted to die for love, asked if there weren't other beautiful causes worth sacrificing your life for. She loves that word: "cause." She uses it a lot, big ideas all over her face. She's crazy.

The girls decided it was worth dying for the country, for the hungry, for the oppressed, and all that nonsense. What they would all like best would be to die digging ditches in India, so the whole world could drink in peace. The professor agreed. That's just like her. She wants us to go fight for a heap of noble causes while she stays quietly at home, watching us depart through her window or from her front stoop or something, her nasty face contorting with emotion as we head off. I think I hate her, her and her face.

If it wasn't enough that they all wanted to die for so many imbecilic reasons—love, liberty, thirst—she also asked leading questions to make us say what she wanted. All the professors are like that. They insist that you parrot back what they think, and if you don't, they call you a green cretin. It's idiotic.

So then the professor told us the story of Galileo. He's an old guy from the past, the one who came up with the idea that the earth moved around the sun. Before then, it was the sun that moved around the earth. When he told the people of his time about this, they were furious. They put him in prison to make him change his mind and say it was the sun that moved. I think they even wanted to kill him.

In the end, Galileo said what everyone wanted him to say. But when he was on his own, he said, "And yet it moves." And it was true. You couldn't stop the earth from moving, but you couldn't say it was happening because it made everybody furious. The professor wanted to know what we would have done in Galileo's place. Would we have said whatever we had to in order to avoid death?

A lot of the girls thought Galileo wasn't very brave. If they'd been Galileo, they would have loudly proclaimed that the earth moves. That made me laugh. First, most of the girls tell on each other to avoid getting punished. And besides, I don't see any of us becoming a great scientist like Galileo one day. But you never know. Maybe Galileo was also very stupid when he went to high school. These are things that nobody ever talks about. But I don't know. What I do know is that Galileo was right. He was a great guy, and a great guy is more useful alive then dead. The professor asks completely idiotic questions.

That day, with her stories of death, I wondered if she might be sick of us all being alive, since she was so intent on making us come up with reasons to die. She must have been tired.

Fanny and I talked about it at recess. Fanny, who's so beautiful, says she's happy to be alive and wants to live for a very long time. She says that ideas are ideas; they don't need us. Me, I didn't say I was happy because it isn't true. But I said that the things that make me feel like dying don't matter to the professor. For example, the times when my grade school teacher said I have a hard heart, and she said that a lot. Or when my father hangs the dog. Everything was stupid, really stupid. Because it's unbearable that you can hang tired old dogs like that, without any consequences. But I couldn't say that to the professor.

Suddenly the first lights of the town appeared. By this time, I hardly expected them anymore.

A wild joy shook me as I saw the lights of the town off in the distance. All at once, it seemed as if I'd been pedaling in the dark for practically fifteen years, to arrive one night amid those lights. Truly, that's what it seemed like to me.

My joy was so immense that I started pedaling like mad. There was nothing more to do but keep going straight ahead. I chanted a song in a very loud voice and rode my bike in zigzags. I was so happy. Before long, I fell again. I fall easily. My knee smarted and I could tell it was bleeding. I made sure my bike still worked. It did. It's a good bicycle, very loyal.

Then I got going again, singing at the top of my lungs and watching all the lights draw nearer. I really wanted to cry.

8

AT LAST, I got there. Out of sheer joy, I came to a stop. I laid my bike down on the grass on the side of the road. I sat down under the streetlight. It's the first streetlight. I've always loved it because it's the first and because it seems lonelier than the others. It belongs neither entirely to the town nor to the country. It bends over passersby with its broad, yellow gaze. I like the other streetlights, too, of course, but I like this one best.

I sat down at its foot and stayed there awhile doing nothing but being there, in all that yellow light. I was tired. Really tired. Tired from everything, and from this cold. All the same, I felt good in this yellow light. I love light and sun. I would like to have always lived in light and sun. I live in the marshes surrounded by streams. That's the way it is because that's where I was born. I would have liked so much to have been born into light and sun.

After a moment I got back up and got on my bicycle again. I had to get back to the high school. I had no idea what time it was.

I paused for a moment to decide which way to go. Ordinarily I take small, deserted roads where nobody can see me riding by, at least, nobody from the high school. My bicycle is in such poor condition, with its missing headlamp, bell, and brakes, that the police might take it away from me. I would rather not make my bike run that risk. I like it a lot, my bicycle. That's why I don't ever want the police to run into us.

Still, after thinking it over, I decided to take the avenues. I wanted so much to see the windows of the stores and their little blinking Christmas lights. Besides, when you've done everything I'd just done, in the midst of all that cold, you definitely have the right to ride through the streets of town with your bicycle. You must have that right.

I rode slowly down the avenues. The stoplights were like a game to me. It was fun. I heard my bicycle whining louder than usual. It's always that way. My bicycle doesn't like the town, it isn't used to it. Poor bicycle. I feel sorry for my bike when I can tell it's so out of its element. The bike and I, we're only at ease when we're all alone.

Arriving on the bridge, I got off my bike. I stepped onto the sidewalk. I knelt at the parapet and looked into the water. The lights of the streetlamps on the bridge were reflected in long trembling columns. I like to watch the lights floating on the water. It's like the water calls to them. I often think that if I threw myself into the water, into one of those columns of light, it would make a great cluster of stars. It would be pretty.

At home, the skies in August are filled with falling stars. That was a very long time ago. When I was little.

I walked slowly. I was in no hurry to get to the high school, now that I was almost there. There was nobody out, nobody at all. With all these useless lights, this desert, this silence pierced by the little cry of the dying salamander, I felt like I was moving through a world of the dead, where preparations for a furtive celebration by ghosts were underway.

Then I hurried up, because the fear was coming back.

Nothing bad could happen to me on this light-drenched bridge. But I was starting to feel afraid. I felt like the high school was retreating deep into an unknown world, into which I would never gain entry again. Thinking like that makes me start suffocating, suffocating for real.

I don't know why, but I remembered something I'd almost forgotten. Something I hardly ever think about.

I remembered the day when we were in a meadow, my mother and me, turning the hay. I remember the brightness of that day, crazy with sunshine and the scent of dried hay, of luminous heat. Maman and I were working quietly, not saying anything, both of us with our pitchforks. I think we were happy. Now I can't be sure.

All of a sudden, Maman stopped and screamed. I ran towards her and saw. In the hay there were chicks torn to pieces. It wasn't the first time I'd seen that. When my father mows the hay, if he comes across a brood of chicks he keeps going all the same, and the chicks who don't have the time to run away are crushed or cut to pieces by the blade of the mower. So we're used to it. But that day, it had just been too beautiful.

My mother gathered up the bits and pieces of the chicks, caked with dried blood, put them in her apron and went to throw them in the stream. I remember the silence and my mother crying. I was very little. Six years old maybe. That sun, and my mother crying. It stays with me.

I don't know what came over me then. I'm often like this. I do crazy things and afterwards don't understand why. I was still so little.

While my mother went to the stream to throw away the torn-up chicks, I took her pitchfork and buried it under a pile of hay, I guess its tines were sticking up. I swear it wasn't on purpose. I was just so little, and didn't understand anything about anything.

When I saw my mother's foot all bloody, I didn't scream or anything. I went quietly to the stream, leaving behind my mother and her wounded foot. I went down to the water through the clusters of wild hazels, into the velvety scent of mint and the water's blue noise. I lay down beneath the surface. The water flowed over me as if I wasn't there.

No sooner had I remembered that than the high school rose before me. I could have exploded with joy, I was so happy to see it. But no.

9

THE DOOR of the high school was locked. It's always locked. That's because of the concierge. If the door was open, he would have nothing to do. It has to be locked.

I rang and the door opened. It opens automatically. The concierge presses a button and it opens. That's clever, I think. The concierge's duties are limited to watching the bell and pressing the button. Since he opens the door for everybody, you might as well leave it open, or not even have a door, it seems to me. It would be exactly the same thing. Or you could set up a bell system that automatically activates the opening of the door without the concierge having to press his button, if you're absolutely determined to have a locked door. But then, the concierge would have nothing to do; and as long as he's there, you've got to find a use for him.

In reality, the concierge at the high school plays another role. He watches and screens the people who arrive. There's a supervisor who does that, too. You're screened twice. The concierge really likes this part of his job. I'm sure that's the reason he likes working at the high school, in spite of that button he has to press all the time. He watches people pass through a little window that has a glass panel in it that he can raise or lower, like at the post office counter. When the girls go by, he doesn't look just anywhere. That is, he doesn't look at faces, eyes or hands, the things that are important to look at. He looks at bottoms. With his fat, red, shrimp's eyes, he slowly watches every bottom that goes by. When he talks, he talks while staring at those bottoms, too. It's disgusting.

This time, I was lucky because it wasn't the concierge who let me in, but his daughter. She's older than me. I don't like her at all, but at least she doesn't stare at people's bottoms.

She's a great big yellow spider, and she trailed me so closely with her eyes that I stopped and stared back at her. I hate it when people stare at me. At that point, she fled her post. That was the right thing to do. Concierges and their families should be done away with.

Back home, we don't need a concierge to screen people who come visit. We don't want to see anybody. Anybody. It's that simple. Also, we've worked it so nobody dares come twice to the place we live, in the middle of the marshes.

In the past, people used to come. The mailman, the mayor, and the police, if we didn't pay our taxes. Sometimes ordinary people too, neighbors. It was kind of amazing that they figured out how to get to us. You've got to cross all the bridges and find the right trails through the marshes, the woods, and the sharp wild grasses, amid bird cries, avoiding wild animals, and in summer, leeches and water snakes. Those who finally make it through all that find a dry, small, stone-ridden mound. Our place.

The dog warns us of our rare visitors. None of our dogs likes strangers, and when our dogs bark, people don't laugh. If the stranger persists and enters the yard of the house, it's simple. He won't find anyone. Of course, we're there. But he won't see us. He can call, shout even, all he likes, with this crazy dog leaping around him, he can sense that we're there watching him, but where are we? We're in the straw, in the ditches, in the trees. And by that time, the stranger is getting spooked by all those eyes, and the howling dog, and hotfoots it out of there, pursued by the barking. That's when we come out of our hiding places and gather on the path to watch him run away. If he sees us, it doesn't matter. He's not coming back. And if he did come back, we'd go back into hiding. Now, thanks to us, nobody dares to come our way anymore. Besides, everyone hates us.

I went to the end of the courtyard to park my bicycle. There were no other bikes there. The girls have parents or friends who drive them to school, or else they take the school bus. Day students have mopeds or new bicycles.

I noticed that it was starting to snow. I was glad. As long as there's no sun, let everything be white with snow. I like that a lot.

Before knocking on the door of the supervisor's office, I took off my dead aunt's raincoat. I'd only thought of it at the last minute. I'd been wearing it for so long that I'd almost forgotten it was on me. As I took it off, I realized why the concierge's daughter had stared at me with her spider's eyes. She must have been wondering what on earth I was wearing. Ordinarily I put on my dead aunt's raincoat at the edge of town when I'm on my way home, and that's where I take it off when I return. It bothered me a little that the concierge's daughter had seen me dressed like that. She takes herself for the daughter of Jesus Christ, no less. That's hardly the case. What is for certain is that her father looks at bottoms. Of course, that isn't her fault.

I rolled up my raincoat into a tight bundle, stuck it under my arm and tried to look nonchalant as I knocked at the door of the supervisor on duty. "Yes!" said the supervisor.

By the tone of her voice I could tell she was not in a joking mood. No supervisor is ever in a joking mood. That's how it is. If they felt like laughing, they wouldn't be supervisors. I walked in. She said, "Your pass?" without even raising her eyes from her book. I could have been anyone and she would have said it the same: "Your pass?"

It's awful.

I'd completely forgotten about the pass. I had the pass, but it wasn't signed. I tried to come up with a lie, but nothing came to me, nothing at all. Usually, lying's pretty easy for me. It's the same old story. When it really counts, I go blank.

So I said, "I forgot to get it signed. At home..."

She raised her head and cut off my improvisation. Her head looked sinister. I don't think I could have come up with anything else. She said, "Oh! It's you, Galla! You've come back?"

That was idiotic. I said, "Yes."

That was idiotic, but so was her question. She said, "You have it, the pass?"

I said, "Yes. It's not signed. I forgot. At home..."

She said, "I know. Just sign it, then sign in on the register. That'll be fine."

Her voice was almost kind. If I'd had more time, it would have irritated me. But I had no time. I hurried to sign, afraid she would change her mind, which would lead to more talking. I thanked her quickly and headed for the door. She added, "Hurry if you want to eat. The meal has begun."

"Yes," I said. "Thanks," and I quickly shut the door. Even on ordinary occasions, I hurry away from the supervisors and professors for fear they'll start talking. Me, I don't want anyone to talk to me or to ask me anything. Especially not at the high school. Here, when a professor or a supervisor speaks to the pupils, it's always to give boring advice or to ask what we're going to be when we grow up. How are we supposed to know? It's obvious that nobody can know that ahead of time. Or else, they pry into your home life. And that I really can't stand. When anyone asks me how things are at home, about my parents, all those sisters of mine, and our life, I walk away without saying a word. And if I do say anything, I make up lies, adding lots of details to make them sound true. When it comes down to it, people here shouldn't be asking me what goes on at home. What happens at home is nobody's business. Me, I never try to find out about other people's lives. For the professors, it's a mania. They are determined to get you to tell them things. Afterwards, they say you're a case for social workers. They love it when people are social cases. You can tell which girls are social cases by the fact that people say their names in a whisper. It's automatic. It's all the same to me. I don't want my name to be whispered. I don't want anyone to talk to me or to talk about me.

I felt glad to have gotten somewhere, someplace warm, and to be about to eat. Glad, too, that the lie about the forgotten pass had worked. When I'm happy like that, I have to do something. On my bicycle I can sing, or do zigzags. Since I couldn't sing at the top of my lungs in the hall, or do zigzags, I tried to slide on the tiles. I gave up quickly. My rubber boots wouldn't slide and besides, my knee hurt a lot. So I took my rolled-up raincoat and threw it into the air, saying as loudly as possible, "So much the better. So much the better."

That didn't mean anything, of course, except that I was

happy, and it was the only thing I could think of to say. I never come up with good ideas.

The third time, my raincoat came unrolled. I stopped throwing it in the air. I remembered that my green smock was in the pocket. Before rolling up my dead aunt's raincoat again, I took out the smock and put it on. It was so crumpled that you'd think I'd balled it up into a pellet. It was terrible. I kept it on all the same, to de-crumple it. Besides, that way it looked less dirty.

I pushed open the glass door of the dining hall. I went in. It sounded subdued. Sunday nights are always sad, and people don't feel much like talking. And, there aren't all that many girls.

When I went in, all the girls turned and looked at me. Immediately, silence fell everywhere. It's always the same. They've never gotten used to seeing me. Me neither, I can't get used to seeing myself, even after all this time. All my joy faded. That was too bad, because I really had been happy to be back. Only, you can't stay happy when you're surrounded by silent faces, when you've got your dead aunt's raincoat under your arm and you're wearing a pathetic crumpled green smock. You can't. So I let all my joy go away. I headed toward the table that wasn't full. At the high school, you've got to fill the tables, and sometimes that means you have to eat with people who take away your appetite. Me, what I would like is to eat at a table by myself, all alone, far from everyone.

I sat down. The girls said, "Good evening."

I replied, "Good evening."

I was about to serve myself some cauliflower when the supervisor arrived. She said, "You've come back?"

I said again, "Yes."

This was starting to get on my nerves. It was idiotic.

"We'll bring you some soup and some ham," the supervisor said.

"Yes," I said.

She left again and I took some cauliflower. There was a lot left. The girls don't like cauliflower much. I started to eat without looking at anyone. I was ravenously hungry. Nobody said a word. I started to get fed up with the silence and all the staring eyes. The whole meal went by that way. I didn't dare eat my fill. That's how I am.

I was glad when at last everyone got up from the table. I noticed that that great big red-headed string bean Lydia was sitting next to me, when she said, displaying all her crowded teeth: "Are you all right?"

"Yes," I said.

I spoke automatically, without taking time to think. Usually I ignore her; she never talks to me except to say mean things. But that wasn't a mean thing, at least, I don't think it was. What's sure is that I was so stunned that I didn't think before I spoke. It's too bad.

I was the last one to leave the dining hall. I took advantage of that to take two pieces of bread, putting one in each pocket of my green smock. I like bread. I planned to eat it before I went to bed, in the bathroom. I do that when I'm very hungry.

In the hall, I saw the two supervisors, the one from the door and the one from the dining hall, talking to each other. I was afraid. Maybe the office supervisor was displeased with the signatures I'd made on the pass and on the register, and was going to tell on me. I'd signed with a swirl of spirals, the way some people do. That's not my real signature, but I couldn't use my real one, because I always sign my leave passes myself. The supervisor would figure that out if she compared the signatures. Maybe I would be expelled from school. I wouldn't want that to happen for anything in the world.

I pretended not to see the supervisors as I went by. I was so afraid. When I'm that afraid, I can hardly walk, my legs get all kinds of tics and tremors. My legs are awful. The supervisors didn't say anything to me. I hurried to join the other girls at the foot of the staircase that leads to the study hall. The study supervisor had us climb the stairs. I was at the end of the line and she was behind me. I hate it when someone's right behind me. Just as I was about to enter the study hall like everyone else, she called out to me. Immediately my legs started twitching. I turned abruptly to the supervisor. Enough of this. After all, it wasn't my fault that I'd signed the pass. I was going to say so, but I didn't have time because she said, "If you'd like to go to sleep right now, you may. You look exhausted."

Without thinking, I said, "Yes."

It wasn't until she held out the dormitory key to me that I really understood. I took it and started running like a fool to the dormitory stairs, both out of joy, and for fear that she might change her mind.

Calmly I climbed the stairs. I thought of my bicycle, alone in the dark in the back of the courtyard. I thought about the leave pass, too. What a stupid lie. I should have signed it the usual way or copied my mother's handwriting. The thought had not even occurred to me. That said, I don't know how my mother signs her name; I'm the one who signs things at home. Like my little sisters' school forms, and my own. Maria, that great big arrogant pest, doesn't want me to touch hers. She signs them herself. That's dumb. If our teacher compared our forms, she would see that the signatures weren't the same. That would make a nice tale to tell at school. Not at home. At home, we don't bother about what happens at school. There are too many of us, and too many other worries. When the teacher, not the mean one, the other one, came to the house—which showed a lot of guts—to talk to my parents and tell them how smart I was, and how I absolutely had to go to the high school so I could have a decent future, and that she'd take care of the applications for the scholarship and all that, my father and my mother said you don't have to be smart to do farm work, and that's true. The teacher wanted to keep on talking, but my father and my mother went off to the streams to cut wood and left her in the yard with the dog. That's how it is at our place. Luckily, the teacher didn't get discouraged. She didn't come back to the house. It was too awful and she wasn't used to it. But she did all the applications just the same. I'm at the high school now.

10

I OPENED the door of the dormitory. I mulled it over a bit then decided to leave the key in the door, on the outside. The key would be fine. And this way, the supervisor wouldn't have to bother me for the key. I didn't want anyone to speak to me. Even to ask me to return a key.

I sat down on my bed. I took out my two pieces of bread. I started to eat them. One bite from the one on the right, one from the one on the left, so neither would feel left out. I like things to be totally fair. For example, I don't like to water the flowers in the garden I planted behind the house. I water them, but I don't like it. All flowers are equally thirsty. But even when I pay close attention, I end up giving less water to one plant than to another. Whatever I do, at least one plant is scanted, which is unbearable. I don't want to give any flower less water than any other. I worry about this all the time. I tell myself it's better to let them all die of thirst than to give one of them less than the others. But I can't do that. I don't want everything to die. It's really terrible. I feel like screaming when I think that everything will always be like this.

I got undressed and took my smock to the showers. I snuck some soap from a toiletry kit and washed it. It was too bad that it wasn't a Saturday. If it had been a Saturday morning, I could have kept the soap and even pocketed some other things. I would have taken them home, it might have made my mother happy. But it was Sunday, and if the girls complained about things going missing, the supervisors would go through everything, and everyone would know it was me. Maybe they'd expel me. I couldn't take a thing, but it wasn't for lack of will.

I spread my green smock over the radiator, stretching it out in every direction so it wouldn't be too wrinkled when it was dry. I would like to be clean and well dressed.

I took a shower. To lather up, I looked for a perfumed soap. I had a variety of choices, which didn't happen often, usually I don't have soap. I took one that smelled of sweet almond. I love the scent of fresh almonds.

In the shower, I let the steaming water flow down over me for a long time while lathering myself over and over. By the end I couldn't see anymore, there was so much steam. I'd never felt so good. I would have liked it to last my whole life, but that wasn't realistic. I sang at the top of my lungs while I rinsed off and while I made my way to bed. It echoed really loudly in the empty hallways. You'd have thought I was at least a hundred people. That made me happy. I kept on singing like that until I was in my bed, under the covers. But there my voice sounded like someone being smothered. It wasn't fun anymore at all. So I stopped. That was better.

I tried to come with up stories to send myself to sleep. I couldn't. My thoughts kept returning to my pass. When something like that is on my mind, I can't think of anything else.

If the supervisor found out I hadn't brought back my signed pass, would she write home to check and see I'd actually been there? Usually she does. She always wants to know what we do when we're away from the high school. Me, I think it's none of her business. It's the parents who ought to ask what goes on at the high school on Sundays. But they couldn't care less. In any case, mine don't. What I do, where I am and all that doesn't matter to them. They never wonder anything about me at all.

The supervisor cares so much about what we get up to on Sundays when we're away from her high school because she imagines that if we don't go to our own homes, we go to some boy's house. That's automatic for her. For example, if she found out that I hadn't gone home, I mean, into the house, and I told her that I'd slept in the straw with my dog then wandered around in the countryside, she wouldn't believe it. Even if I explained it all to her thoroughly, she wouldn't believe it, because it would never occur to her to leave the high school to go sleep with a dog in the straw in a barn. She would think I had gone off to see a boy. That's a completely ridiculous idea, but what can you do? If a supervisor is determined to believe that you've gone off to see a boy, you can't convince her otherwise.

As for the letter she'd send home, that didn't worry me. First off, my parents wouldn't care where I'd been on Sunday. Plus, they'll never get the letter. They never get any letters. The mailman is still spooked from the days when he used to try to come to the house to deliver our mail. So he stops my little sisters or me on the school path to give us our letters. At first, the little ones and I would take time to consider each letter, its envelope, its handwriting, its contents, before gathering beside a stream to decide its fate. Soon we understood that we had to drown *all* the letters and that's how it would always be. We decided to drown them immediately, without wasting any time thinking about it. This drives the mayor, the police, and the tax collector completely insane. They don't understand where their letters end up, and they have to lie in wait for my father when he goes to the village. In any case, the supervisor can write letters to my father until the end of the world if she wants. He'll never get them. They'll be drowned in the cold waters of the marshes. Obviously, I can't tell her that. Too bad for her.

I thought about it a little more, then decided there was no need to worry about the unsigned pass. I went back to thinking up other things to make me fall asleep. Nothing came to mind. I don't have much imagination. When I was little, I had plenty. Every night I would tell myself the same story.

When I was little, this is what I told myself: My parents, all my sisters, the stones in the earth, the sullen waters of the marshes, none of it matters to me. Because these are not my parents. My real parents are rich. They live in vast mansions, they eat meat and warm bread all day, wear shoes even in summer, and coats in winter. They have warm stockings, they're clean, and they smell good. They sleep in soft beds, one bed each, on beautiful sheets embroidered with horns of plenty, without the smell of babies or anything. All day long, you can walk into their house without shame, the house gleams and sings. And all day long, they love one another and they love me; all day long they laugh at everyone because they aren't afraid of anybody and everyone loves them. My real parents lost me. They're looking for me everywhere and they're desperate. One day they'll find me again, they'll take me far away from the fogs of the marshes, to lands where the days are gilded with sunshine, where you sleep at night cradled in the blue of the waves of the sea. I don't care that there are so many stones, that we live buried behind streams, that my mother cries, that my father beats me. It's all the same to me. A day will come when my real parents will take me far away, into the light and heat.

Every night I would dream of that moment. I waited. I don't know when I stopped waiting. Or maybe I waited too long. I don't know. One night I dreamed of a day when I'd have a lot of money and we would buy serene, beautiful land. Now I'm at the high school.

I tried to tell myself a story about the land we'll own one day. I couldn't do it. I quit thinking about it.

11

SUDDENLY, a clanking noise rose up around me. I thought
of my father moving around the barn. If he found me lying
in the dog's straw bed, he'd get out his cattle prod. I made a
superhuman effort to raise myself. I didn't want to die at the
bottom of a hole, crushed like a mouse. I wanted to die, but
not like that. I made another superhuman effort, and at last
was able to get up.

The supervisor was standing by my bed, rapping the metal
bedstead with her bunch of keys. She said, "Hurry up. It's
late," as she always does.

I said, "Yes. I know," which wasn't true.

She left. I sat in bed a moment collecting my thoughts.
My heart was racing. Sometimes I think I have a completely
crazy heart. I looked around the dormitory a little. It was
empty, all the beds were unmade. The girls must have been
in the bathroom. Usually I'm the first, to make sure I get a
spot. There aren't enough sinks in my high school. I decided
I'd go to the sinks later. I got up. I folded my blankets and
my sheets. The supervisors want us to fold everything every
morning. At noon we go up again and make the beds. It's
ridiculous, so much fuss about a bed. But the supervisors all
decided it would be that way. They're maniacs. And they
never laugh.

I started dressing and went to the sinks to look for my

green smock. I didn't worry if it would still be on the radiator. I've tried to lose it many times, with no success. It was there, but on the floor and pretty rumpled. I shook it out noisily, like my mother does with the sheets, then put it on. Washing it had brightened the green, my smock shone and gave off the scent of soap. I like the smell of soap. Then I went to the bathroom.

Only a few girls were left. Dirty sinks disgust me. The girls don't clean up after themselves. That great big string bean Lydia, who always gets up last, said "Good morning" to me, and I said "Good morning" in turn, while water flowed from the sink. I splashed water all over my face. That woke me up and immediately I felt glad to be back. Really glad. I raised my head and amused myself by listening to the water drops trickling down my skin and falling from my chin. When I'm happy I like to do that. When I'd finished I opened my eyes and there was great big Lydia, still in front of me.

She flashed all her teeth, big as almonds, and said: "What did you memorize for your recitation?"

It took me a while to understand what she was talking about. I opened my mouth to answer, but I had nothing to say. So I turned my back on that yellow string bean and dried my face. She left. Besides, I never talk to her. At first, I didn't know any better. I would answer when she talked. But then she would mock what I'd said in front of the others. For example, the time when she asked what my parents do. I hate it when people ask me what my parents do. It had made me angry. I said, "My parents prospect for gold in Alaska."

That's not true of course. But she shouldn't have asked me what my parents do and all that nonsense. That's why I said: "My parents prospect for gold in Alaska." And also because I was thinking of people hunting nuggets. It wasn't true that my parents prospected for gold, but it could have been true. After I told that story, great big Lydia made fun of me, and now I don't answer her questions. Even when she's nice. With her, you never know. I don't answer anymore.

I combed my hair without looking at myself in the mirrors. I don't like looking at myself. Then I went and locked myself in a bathroom stall while I waited for the breakfast bell.

I thought about the recitation. We have French class the first hour of school, and the professor wants us, all of us, to have memorized something to recite. You can choose anything you like, it's all the same to her, as long as you've memorized something. I'd completely forgotten. Some days I lose it. Right now, for instance, I knew very well that I was at the high school because I felt so happy to be back. But it hadn't quite registered, not really, since I'd forgotten about the recitation, the classes, the professors, and even Fanny. That's how I get when I lose it. I'm aware of something, and at the same time I'm not. It's terrible to be like me.

It was too late to memorize something new. So I searched my brain for a poem I already knew. I know a lot of poems by heart, a hundred, maybe more. The teacher at my grade school, the one who was nice, lent me her books. I thought for a while. I couldn't remember anything at all. Finally, the only one that came to me was: "Forehead on the windowpane like mourners keeping vigil." I was happy because I like that one a lot and because I would be able to go calmly into the schoolyard with Fanny. Thinking of Fanny filled me with sunlit joy. She is so marvelous.

The bell rang. I decided to leave the bathroom stall. The girls were walking to the stairs in their well-ironed pink smocks with their made-up faces. The science professor doesn't want us to use makeup. She says that before long our skin will look old and wrinkled if we paint our faces like that. The professors use makeup, of course. But they already have wrinkled skin. It doesn't matter anymore. Me, I don't make myself up. For one thing, I don't have any makeup. And for another, if I used it I'd look even more like a clown. Nobody would take my made-up face seriously.

At the table, I was seated again next to Lydia. I didn't talk to her. Nobody spoke to me. Lydia included. She must have understood. It isn't because of her huge teeth that are always flashing in the air, or because of her legs like giant match-sticks. It's that she's mean. I drank café au lait and ate two enormous pieces of bread with jam. I'm always hungry. I've got to eat, I'm always hungry. I think it's a habit. For fourteen years, I've been in the habit of being hungry. Now I keep it up, even when it's not needed.

We all got up. We went out to the schoolyard. The girls shouted as they ran. There was snow everywhere. I knew that but I'd completely forgotten. I ran too, but without jostling anyone, I didn't feel like it.

The day students and the boarders who come back to school Monday morning had already dirtied the snow with their footsteps. Some of the students were circling the court-yard, going over their lessons as they walked, some threw snowballs, some packed snow to make a snowman. I looked over the wall at a sky of a gray that was almost as pale as the snow. All of a sudden I felt really happy. I walked around looking for Fanny. You can see her from far away, with her hair like the sun. The cold invaded my feet through the rub-ber of my boots. For a while I had fun pretending I was walking barefoot in the snow. Often I think that one day I'll walk like that into a desert of snow, deeper and deeper.

I will walk for a very long time in all that glittering silence. Then I will disappear in the snow, and everything will be as if I had never existed.

I saw Fanny at last. She was throwing snowballs with the other girls in our class. How beautiful she was with her laughing face! If I had been born in the sun, amid the rolling blue waves of the sea, I would have been beautiful like that.

I walked toward the place where Fanny was playing, trying to look like a passerby who strolls nonchalantly, lost in thought, paying no attention to his surroundings. I was thinking about all the dead nuns we walked over every day.

Before it was a high school, my high school was a convent. It still has the vaulted hallways, the chapel, and the thick pillars; and in the dormitories, colorful stained-glass windows filled with scenes that keep you from ever seeing the light of day. There's a high wall around the high school studded with broken glass. Most important, in the schoolyard, the nuns are still there. The schoolyard used to be the cemetery. They say that every day the nuns came there to dig their graves. Every day. Me, what I'd like to know is what they did once they'd finished digging, if they didn't die straightaway. Surely they didn't dig another one. One would be enough, and you couldn't dig one for anyone else, because each one of them was supposed to tend her own. And surely they didn't fill them back in and start all over again. It would have been idiotic, or awkward, if they happened to die before they finished, that's something you can't foresee. So, what did they do when they finished digging their graves, if they didn't die straightaway?

Afterwards, when the convent became a high school, they

didn't remove the dead nuns. They simply tarred over the cemetery and turned it into a playground. Now the nuns are at rest with their faces covered with tar and we—we walk on top of them. It's unbearable. In the schoolyard, whether we walk quietly or play, we are trampling the stomachs and faces of dead nuns covered with tar.

My heart felt heavy.

Suddenly, Fanny was there. From a distance, she said, "Galla!" And me, I said, "Fanny!" and we started running. When we were face to face we stopped. She stared at me, and I stared back, at her face filled with sunshine and laughter. We didn't know what to say to each other. When we meet, Fanny and I, we're so happy that we forget what to say. We walked a little and I took care to put my feet only on fresh clumps of snow. And then Fanny said, "You came?"

I looked at her. I saw that her face was sad. Golden and sad. I said, "Yes."

The bell rang. I said, "At recess, we'll make a snowman as high as the sky."

I didn't want her to look sad. Afterwards, surrounded by the others, we walked to class without saying anything. We were at the back of the line, next to each other. As we went in, Fanny said, "I'm happy you're here. I was thinking about you so much. So, so much. Could you feel that I was thinking about you?"

I said, "Yes." But it wasn't true, of course. That made me sad. I thought that, one day, someone like Fanny, someone who genuinely liked me a whole lot, and who hadn't ever done anything to anybody, might think that much about me, and on that very day, terrible things would happen. But when nobody and nothing thinks about me, what will happen then? It felt like all my joy at being back in the high school next to Fanny was about to crumble away, leaving nothing.

I sat down at my desk in the back of the classroom. Fanny sat beside me—that's her spot. Some desks were empty, because of the snow, no doubt. For no reason, I thought, so much the better. I often think dumb things for no reason. The professor kept her fur coat on. She has a rabbit fur coat. That disgusts me. At our place, rabbits die every year because of epidemics. The professor said, "Oh, it's cold. Oh, it's cold" in her high-pitched voice. Instantly, all the girls smiled at her. It's the same every time. When she comes back, saying: "Some air. Some air. It stinks in here," the girls smile at her, windmilling their arms. Always. I think if she said, "You are stupid little hyenas," or "You are pink cretins"—which is true—the girls would still keep smiling. They are stupid and so is the professor. When I see that, I hate them all. In any case, I never smile. Except at Fanny, of course.

The professor took out her grade book and began making the girls do the recitations. The girls recited. It was boring because I know all those poems. When it was done, the professor said, "Who will volunteer?"

I hesitated a bit, then, because nobody got up, decided to do it. I wanted to say "Forehead on the windowpane like mourners keeping vigil," again, and that way I'd get a good grade, which could be important if I got in trouble because of the pass. I went up to the podium. The professor likes us to recite at the podium, facing the others, whom she calls "the auditors," because she doesn't like to use the words everyone else uses. I did it the way she likes and looked straight ahead, at Fanny. Some girls recite with their eyes on the ceiling, others look at their feet. Me, I look at Fanny, who looks at me.

I was about to start reciting when a terrible silence seemed to swallow me up. All the girls were staring at me. They used to do that at the beginning, because of my green smock. But over time, they stopped, and now whenever I recite they just go on drawing on their desks or on a piece of paper. My heart began beating wildly. I wondered what was wrong with me. All the same, I looked at the professor, who said nothing, and I began: "Forehead on the windowpane like mourners keeping vigil."

And then I couldn't remember any more. Nothing. I searched for a moment and everybody watched and kept quiet. The only thing that came back to me was the ending. So I said it, very fast so it would end:

> I look for you beyond waiting
> I look for you beyond myself
> And I love you so much, I no longer know
> Which of us two is gone.

I waited. The professor said, "Thank you."

She always says that. Whether you recite well or badly, she says that, in her high-pitched voice: "Thank you."

And she gives us a six or a five. I can't stand it, I really can't. So I said, "I didn't have time to learn a recitation. I had to help my mother work."

It was completely idiotic to say that, but she annoyed me so much with her "Thank you." And I couldn't explain to her that I'd had to sleep in the straw with my dog. She wouldn't have believed me.

She said, "I know, Galla. But it's good that you wanted to recite. Thank you."

I returned to my place angrier than before. I sat next to Fanny. Another girl was reciting. Fanny curled her hand into a shell in front of her mouth so nobody could hear. She said, "Why did you say that? She knows that your mother is dead."

I looked at Fanny and I said, "My mother is not dead."

Fanny looked at me too and said, "But your sister? She telephoned with the news. You had just left. She said that your mother died in the marshes."

Me, I said, "My sister is a jealous pest. She wanted to play a trick on me. She wanted me to come back home."

Fanny said, "That's a terrible trick."

I said, "My sister is a horrible, filthy pest."

Fanny thought then said, "Did your mother know? What she said?"

I said, "She didn't say anything."

Fanny said, "What are you going to do now? Everyone thinks your mother died in the marshes. The supervisor warned the girls that if they behaved unkindly to you they would be sent to the principal's office."

I said, "What business is it of hers?" And then I lifted my head and tried to listen to the professor, who was reading aloud the story of Rodrigo and Chimène. Then I thought a little about my situation.

I thought about it for a while. In the end, I got up, and without saying anything to anyone, I walked out.

12

I WENT to the back of the courtyard to be with my bicycle. Not the courtyard with the nuns, another one that they call the courtyard of honor, because it's in front of the high school. I like this courtyard because of the cedars, the beautiful cedars, very thick and very tall. Fanny says their name is cedars of Lebanon because they come from Lebanon, and endless cedar forests grow in Lebanon. I would have liked to know if the dead nuns in the courtyard had been permitted to stroll and sit beneath the cedars in the court of honor. We weren't. But they, when they were alive, while they were digging their graves every day, did they walk slowly with the broad calm branches of the cedars spreading before them? If that was permitted, it must have consoled them a little for the graves they were digging to die in. It's hard to know what the dead nuns thought when they were alive.

I found my bicycle where I had put it, surrounded by shiny bikes and mopeds. My bicycle looked completely miserable and lost. I grabbed it very quickly to get it away from all that. I walked across the courtyard to the gate. I was lucky, it was open. Delivery people were carrying boxes into the high school. The concierge was right behind them, looking at their buttocks. I went through quietly with my bike. I pictured myself on the first day I came to school, all alone with my old bicycle, my green smock that I'd just finished, and which I had ironed three or four times, and my mother's big shopping bag. There were a lot of people, girls, parents, cars, lots of people, really, and lots of noise, and me, I didn't know anybody, and I entered the place with my old bicycle, my green smock and my black bag. That was a really long time ago.

In the street, a truck was unloading sand onto the snow. Men were talking, because of all the white stuff, maybe. Cars passed, rarely and slowly. I walked, pushing my bike on the sandy road, and sometimes the cars had to slow to a crawl behind me while they waited for the car in the opposite lane to pass. That made me want to laugh. If they knew who I was, would the cars take such precautions? I don't know. They don't have the right to knock me down, of course. But sometimes they do it all the same. That happened to Maman one day when she went into town. There was no snow that day. The car simply bumped into her and my mother fell down. Nothing serious happened to her. Just a scraped leg and face. Maman went back home by bike as usual. A few days later, she gave birth to the baby she'd been expecting for five months. I'm the one who helped her, Maria never wants to do that, the dirty pest. Maman was in a lot of pain, she needed help. Afterwards, she told me to go throw the dead baby into the stream. I put it in a big pan to carry it into the marshes. It was very pretty, like a big doll, already finished, its little ribs tracing fine lines under its skin. I looked and I saw that it was a boy. That was funny.

I put it in a hole in the marshes in the middle of a lot of tall grasses. But the birds must have found it. When I came back to the house, Maman was feeling better. She wasn't sorry about the baby, of course; she had had too many of them already. I didn't tell her that it was a boy. I didn't tell anybody.

When my mother told this story to that hyena, Aunt Gina, Aunt Gina told her she could have asked for damages from the car. She said she would have got a lot of money because of the lost baby. My mother said nothing. When my aunt was far away, she said, "People like us can't do that. Those aren't things for us." And it's true that I would have found it weird to get money like that, all of a sudden, without working for it. We could have bought good land at last, far from the marshes and the mists. Me, I don't know.

I stopped for a moment on the bridge. I watched the water flow. It had a beautiful color, a tranquil, creamy green. I thought about how pretty a landscape with water can be, except for marshes like ours, where savage waters lurk amid sullen grasses. I was sorry to miss the sight of the splintered light of the lampposts spilling over the water. They had turned off the streetlights. It was daytime, the light was all white and blue. At our place, the dawn light is often white and blue and creamy because of the mists that cloak the ghostly trees. My father says that all water rises to the sky as vapor. Sometimes at our place, the sky, the earth, and the trees blend together. You can't tell them apart. The mad birds shriek, get lost, and drown.

After the bridge, I took side roads so policemen wouldn't catch me with my bicycle. We can't pass by unnoticed, the two of us, it always makes its sad little squeaking noise, even when I lead it by the hand. I would have liked to stop and look in the shop windows. I could stand motionless in front of them for hours, dreaming up stories. In front of the groceries and snack bars of my village, you can't dream. But, for my bicycle's sake, it was better to take the side roads.

The warmth of the high school was fading and I started to feel very cold. I'm always cold, but at the high school, I felt warm at last, as if by a miracle. My dead aunt's raincoat had stayed behind in the dormitory cloakroom. I wondered what would happen to it. Would somebody take it and help themselves to it? Hardly likely. Surely nobody would take it, unless maybe to disguise themselves and pretend they were me. On this cold morning, it was sad to think about a raincoat so ugly that nobody would ever want it. Truly it was sad, on this cold morning.

There was nobody on the street, not anywhere. Even the dogs were dozing in the warmth of all those locked houses. The emptiness was so absolute that it seemed like nobody was alive anywhere. If I went into those houses, there would be nobody inside, even the basements and the attics would be empty. Yet trash cans stood like sentinels before the gates of the front yards. Here one trash can, here two trash cans. People had taken them out, other people would come to empty them. The thought almost made me laugh. The only sign of life in these deserted streets was the trash cans. Trash cans were the residents of these fine houses. I thought again of my father who always says that rich people produce a lot of garbage. As I walked past these houses with my bicycle I entertained myself by saying out loud "Rich," or "Less rich," depending on the number of trash cans. But maybe I was mistaken. There's no telling. I would have liked to be a mad dog so I could bark in front of those doors, bark terrifyingly, to make someone come out.

Finally I reached the town's last streetlight. It was unlit, useless. I felt sorry for it, and for my dead aunt's raincoat. I looked at the long street that vanished into the town and it reminded me of Nicole. She wasn't in class this morning. Had her mother succeeded in dying? And she, what was she doing? I wanted very much to return to the high school to find out. Was Nicole's mother dead, and what would become of Nicole? It was unbearable not to know. Nonetheless, I didn't go back to the high school. There were too many streets to retrace, with the trash cans guarding the houses, and the dogs shut up inside. I waited at the foot of the last streetlight, hoping somebody might come whom I could ask. Nobody came. I wanted to ask: When a woman dies and she has a child in her womb, what becomes of the child? Does it die too? Does it keep on living for a while, nourishing itself from the dead woman? What becomes of a living child in the womb of a dead woman?

I wanted to scream so somebody would come and tell me. Truly, I wanted to scream. But nobody would have heard me. There was nothing there, I knew, except for the steetlight, my bicycle with its squeak of a dying salamander, and me. None of the three of us knew. And if somebody did come and I asked:"What becomes of a living child in the womb of a dead woman?" would he start screaming and run away? I don't know. I just don't know.

I stayed there, on the road, with the unlit lamppost and the bicycle. I wondered: what do you do, for no reason, if there is nobody?; what do you do?, because I was so fed up with everything, and there was nothing to do about it. I know very well that that's the way it is.

13

I LEFT the lamppost. My bicycle trailed its unhappy little cry all the way down the silent road. I straddled it and pedaled with caution. I was afraid. My knee hurt so much that I didn't dare make my bike risk another fall. Poor bicycle, alone with me on this road, and poor knee. My bicycle and my knee seemed to carry all the weight of the sickly sky. I felt an irresistible urge to cry come over me, on this heavy road that stretched out everywhere. And so I cried.

I pedaled harder. I remembered Fanny and her laughing face. Me, on my old rusty bicycle, my smock so green against the white road, and Fanny throwing snowballs in the school-yard, on top of the dead nuns trapped in tar. Fanny played, her face shining with laughter. The sobs escaped on their own, I heard them alongside my bicycle's cries. It doesn't take much. Lydia's teeth, enormous, always flashing. Teeth that were too big and looked like peeled almonds. She couldn't do anything about it. Teeth like almonds or a smock that's too green. It doesn't take much.

I stopped crying. It was ridiculous. Nothing was strong enough, not tears, not laughter, to fight horrible doomed teeth, a dying bicycle, the whole crumbled world. Nothing. Crying was so stupid that I felt like laughing.

I kept on walking in the cold. A long time after, when the road was about to pass beyond the river, I stopped. I picked up my bike and walked down the riverbank to the path by the water. I sat down, my bicycle lay in the snow beside me. On nice days, fishermen must sit there, calmly watching their lines. I would have liked to be a calm fisherman sitting in the sun, my line beside me, if only just once. But it was too cold, cold as ice, and even when I closed my eyes I couldn't dream that I was a calm fisherman in the sun.

When I opened my eyes, I saw that my bicycle was slowly sliding down the snow toward the river. It had stopped making its salamander cry. I could have pulled it back. But no.

I watched it slowly sink into the water. There wasn't even a splash. After a moment, the water rolled over it, as calmly as if it had never existed. I wondered if leeches lived in the river, like in our marshes. When I was little, my father told us about a man who'd been stranded in the treacherous waters of the marshes. Leeches had sucked up all his blood. Hundreds of leeches, as big as fists, my father said. Their cold mouths, stuck all over his skin, had sucked out all of the man's blood, and afterwards they couldn't save him. I would have liked to know if there were leeches in all the water holes of our marshes.

I walked. For a long time I walked in the cold of the earth and the sky.

Snow began to fall, tenderly, silently. I became a block of ice, thrown off balance by the drifting snow. It snowed without end and I walked without end.

And then, at the end of the night, I arrived at the edge of marshes stiff with frost under a cold, starry sky. I thought of Daisy, sleeping in her bed, the puppy in the hollow of her soft belly. I said to myself: she's a good mother, Daisy. She's a good mother.

AN INTERVIEW WITH INÈS CAGNATI*

Moderated by Pierre-Pascal Rossi

PIERRE-PASCAL ROSSI: Inès Cagnati, this year you brought
 out a very fine collection of short stories, published
 by Julliard, which is why you are here today: *Les
 Pipistrelles*. It's your fourth work, and for the previous
 three you won three literary prizes. In 1973, you won
 the Prix Roger Nimier for *Le Jour de congé*, published
 by Denoël; in 1977 you won the Prix des Deux Magots
 for *Génie la folle*—again, with Denoël; and in 1980,
 Mosé, ou Le Lézard qui pleurait won the Prix Spécial
 des Bibliothèques—again, from Denoël. So, with *Les
 Pipistrelles*, do you expect to get a fourth literary prize
 for your fourth book?

INÈS CAGNATI: What a question.

P-PR: Would you like to?

IC: Everyone likes getting awards, but ... if it doesn't get
 one, it doesn't matter.

P-PR: But to get three in a row for three consecutive works,
 that's really impressive. Wasn't that hard for you to
 deal with?

IC: No, no.

*This interview aired on *Hôtel*, a French literary television program, on No-
vember 23, 1989.

135

P-PR: It seemed natural to you?

IC: I wouldn't say natural, but I was preoccupied by other things...There's life and then there's books.

P-PR: So, the prizes were just something extra.

IC: The prizes were just something extra.

P-PR: So, the basics: But you were born in France, you're French, but your origins—

IC: No, I was naturalized French, that's very different.

P-PR: But you were born in France.

IC: Yes.

P-PR: But your parents were Italian immigrants.

IC: Yes.

P-PR: Where were they from?

IC: My father was from the region of Treviso, my mother from the region of Vicenza. So both of them were from the north.

P-PR: In most of the stories in *Les Pipistrelles*, the narrator is a little girl who herself is the daughter of poor immigrant parents, peasants who settled in France. You get the impression, the feeling, reading these stories, that you yourself were very marked by this childhood, by the world of childhood, which is very much your universe.

IC: That's to be expected, I'd say, because to be a child, it seems to me, is to be born apart, misunderstood by adults, who want to treat you like a miniature woman or little man... which isn't right, and which already constitutes one kind of strangeness for the child. Then beyond that, we had the misfortune of being foreigners, and always being regarded as strangers.

P-PR: There's a sentence by the father in *Les Pipistrelles*, I don't know if it's something your own father said, but the father who's an Italian immigrant who's moved to France, says of his neighbor peasants, who are French, "They are foreigners, but they're at home."

IC: My father didn't say that, I did.

P-PR: It's a very nice sentence; he thinks the French are strangers, "but they're at home."

IC: Yes, but worse... For example, when you think of the Polish Russians, who are also their neighbors, they are even stranger than you, there's a whole hierarchy of foreignness; they're foreign because of their language, because of [the distance of their home country, like Siberia] ... so there's a whole hierarchy among foreigners.

P-PR: In your life in France, did you feel very strongly in your childhood this condition of being a daughter of immigrants, of being a foreigner?

IC: Yes, always. Even now. And on top of that, when my parents had me naturalized, that was a tragedy, because I was not French. I wasn't Italian anymore either. So I was nothing.

P-PR: Do you still feel like a foreigner today?

IC: Yes.

P-PR: You don't feel French?

IC: No. Only my son is French.

P-PR: But French is your language.

IC: No, my mother tongue is Italian.

P-PR: But you write in French.

IC: Yes, and I'm even a professor of French language and literature.

P-PR: But you learned French late.

IC: One year, at school.

P-PR: One year at school. Before school you only spoke Italian at home?

IC: Yes, we knew nobody. And worse, the only people we went to see were foreign. As I said of the French—foreigners but at home—they were foreigners, at home, but of another commune, so strangers, too . . . even more so, from my point of view.

P-PR: Was childhood a happy time for you?

IC: For me, unhappy, completely unhappy.

P-PR: Why? Because of this solitude, because of this incomprehension of the adult world?

IC: Maybe it was just that I lived badly. I don't know. You're all alone. Nobody understands you, they demand things of you that you don't understand, particularly when you don't speak the language.

P-PR: That's a theme that emerges in many of these stories: the solitude and the cruelty of this solitude, the difficulty of this solitude. Children are isolated, as are the elderly, because they're abandoned.

IC: Or crazy people.

P-PR: Or crazy people.

IC: Yes. They're not like other people, they don't react like other people, they're not perceived to be like other people. So, it's a shame, life is crazy for them.

P-PR: This is a world that you inhabited and felt very strongly?

IC: Yes. Even now.

P-PR: Even now.

IC: Yes.

P-PR: But your anchor point, the value you hold to most firmly, seems to be the family unit.

IC: Yes, because it's the only foothold you have in the world, the familial unit, with the father and the mother, even if they did not do for you what they could have done ...

P-PR: Without which you're alone.

IC: Without which you're alone. You're always alone in any case, but you feel it less in the family setting. In truth, my true family right now is my son, perhaps because I made him.

P-PR: Your son is foremost.

IC: Yes.

P-PR: Is that not excessive?

IC: Not if I don't make him feel it that way, no.

P-PR: Yet there's another source of joy, or comfort, or plea-
      sure, and even sensuality [in your writing], and that's
      the pleasure of nature, which you describe magnifi-
      cently well, almost sensually; one feels that you rejoice
      in sensuality in your descriptions of nature. I can't
      resist reading a short passage:

> We arrive, out of breath, at the banks of a stream
> of cool, flowing water that traces fine lines on
> the sand of the riverbed, we sit on moss, our
> backs leaning against a poplar to eat our bunches
> of grapes, mine is a little crushed, I'd gripped it
> too hard as we ran; we wade in the water, inhal-
> ing the scent of the fresh herbs, not the same as
> the ones back in the field, except for the pep-
> permint; pushing aside the water skeeters, cup-
> ping our hands like shells to take a drink.

      There's truly a sense of rejoicing in contact with
      nature in these stories.

IC: I still feel that. It's not just a question of memories.
      It's the same today.

P-PR: You live in the countryside now?

IC: More or less.

P-PR: Do you feel a need for the countryside?

IC: It's where I feel at home. In town I feel unhappy, un-
      happy. With the people in town I feel still unhappier.

P-PR: With everyone?

IC: Yes.

P-PR: You've never had encounters in cities that felt a little bit friendly and warm?

IC: Sure, but most of those have been chance encounters.

P-PR: Fortuitous.

IC: Yes, but it's fine with me if they're fortuitous. Whereas in the countryside, people know me when they see me, and come along with me when I go on walks. That's just how it is.

P-PR: Is writing a comfort to you? A means of liberating yourself from certain things?

IC: It is terrible to write certain things.

P-PR: It's hard to write?

IC: Yes. Certain things are hard to write, for example ... it didn't happen in this book, except for in the last story, "The Woman with No Name." But, in my novel *Génie la Folle*—you haven't read that one I think?

P-PR: No.

IC: There's a passage, I don't know how I managed to write it. It's about a little boy whose cousins made him drink from a wine cask when he was only eighteen months old. He died. Even to write it ... [*Gasps, remembering the horror.*] He was barely off the breast.

P-PR: Yet there's a lot of cruelty in the stories in *Les Pipistrelles*. Is that hard? Is it hard to write about cruel things?

IC: Very. Even things that sound banal, as with the lizard [I write about].

P-PR: Yes.

IC: Because writing takes time.

P-PR: We'll speak later of the lizard. But there's a question I'd like to ask you. You've just published your fourth book, you've already received three literary prizes, but you've been writing for a long time. The first book was in 1973, the next one in 1977, the next in 1980, and now one in 1989. In other words, in almost twenty years of writing, you've published four works, that's not very much. Is that because you write slowly, or because you publish little of what you write, or because you take great pains with your writing?

IC: It's because if I have nothing to say, I say nothing. And I find there are many more occasions to keep quiet than to speak. And if you have nothing to say, it's best to keep quiet.

P-PR: Are there periods when you don't write at all?

IC: Yes.

P-PR: You don't miss it?

IC: No.

P-PR: What's after *Les Pipistrelles*, anything else coming up?

IC: I have half a book.

P-PR: Half a book?

IC: [*Laughs.*] That I have to finish.

P-PR: So, we'll have to wait another five years?

IC: Maybe not. [*Laughs.*]

P-PR: In any case, we have this magnificent book. I'll remind you of the title, *Les Pipistrelles*, by Inès Cagnati, published by Julliard. And to conclude our Inès Cagnati interview, Maria will read for us the ending of this magnificent short story, which is extremely cruel, yet also, as you said earlier, banal, about the lizards—two elderly people who have invited their children over for dinner, and are disappointed because the children only come for the meal, then leave very quickly, when the old folks had been looking forward to their visit for a very long time.

IC: Yes.

P-PR: And a little question I had forgotten. As one sign of your originality, rather than citing other authors— poems at the outset of your works—you cite them here at the end of your stories. Why?

IC: I think it has more meaning that way.

P-PR: So that it can serve as a kind of conclusion?

IC: Yes, in a way. If you highlight them before the story has begun, the reader doesn't know what you've talked about yet. I think it's better for them to look up the sentence or the sentences at the end—like in a movie when you watch the credits.

OTHER NEW YORK REVIEW CLASSICS

For a complete list of titles, visit www.nyrb.com or write to:
Catalog Requests, NYRB, 435 Hudson Street, New York, NY 10014

RENATA ADLER Speedboat
LEOPOLDO ALAS His Only Son *with* Doña Berta
KINGSLEY AMIS Lucky Jim
IVO ANDRIĆ Omer Pasha Latas
EVE BABITZ I Used to Be Charming: The Rest of Eve Babitz
HONORÉ DE BALZAC The Memoirs of Two Young Wives
VICKI BAUM Grand Hotel
WALTER BENJAMIN The Storyteller Essays
EMMANUEL BOVE My Friends
MILLEN BRAND The Outward Room
SIR THOMAS BROWNE Religio Medici and Urne-Buriall
LEONORA CARRINGTON Down Below
EILEEN CHANG Love in a Fallen City
FRANÇOIS-RENÉ DE CHATEAUBRIAND Memoirs from Beyond the Grave, 1768–1800
COLETTE The Pure and the Impure
BARBARA COMYNS The Juniper Tree
ALBERT COSSERY The Jokers
JÓZEF CZAPSKI Lost Time: Lectures on Proust in a Soviet Prison Camp
AGNES DE MILLE Dance to the Piper
MARIA DERMOÛT The Ten Thousand Things
ELAINE DUNDY The Dud Avocado
FÉLIX FÉNÉON Novels in Three Lines
BENJAMIN FONDANE Existential Monday: Philosophical Essays
SANFORD FRIEDMAN Conversations with Beethoven
MAVIS GALLANT The Cost of Living: Early and Uncollected Stories
LEONARD GARDNER Fat City
THÉOPHILE GAUTIER My Fantoms
ÉLISABETH GILLE The Mirador: Dreamed Memories of Irène Némirovsky by Her Daughter
FRANÇOISE GILOT Life with Picasso
NATALIA GINZBURG Family Lexicon
JEAN GIONO Hill
A.C. GRAHAM Poems of the Late T'ang
JULIEN GRACQ Balcony in the Forest
HENRY GREEN Back
VASILY GROSSMAN Stalingrad
LOUIS GUILLOUX Blood Dark
ELIZABETH HARDWICK The New York Stories of Elizabeth Hardwick
ALFRED HAYES My Face for the World to See
RUSSELL HOBAN Turtle Diary
JANET HOBHOUSE The Furies
DOROTHY B. HUGHES In a Lonely Place
RICHARD HUGHES A High Wind in Jamaica
MAUDE HUTCHINS Victorine
DARIUS JAMES Negrophobia: An Urban Parable
TOVE JANSSON The Summer Book
UWE JOHNSON Anniversaries
ERICH KÄSTNER Going to the Dogs: The Story of a Moralist
HELEN KELLER The World I Live In
WALTER KEMPOWSKI All for Nothing
DEZSŐ KOSZTOLÁNYI Skylark